STEVIE-GIRL AND THE PHANTOM OF CRYBABY BRIDGE

ANN SWANN

5 PRINCE PUBLISHING

STEVIE-GIRL AND THE PHANTOM OF CRYBABY BRIDGE

THE PHANTOM SERIES – BOOK THREE

Ann Swann

5 PRINCE PUBLISHING & BOOKS, LLC

PO Box 971 Golden, CO 80402-0971

www.5PrinceBooks.com

Digital ISBN: 978-1-63112-208-8

Print ISBN: 978-1-63112-209-5

Published by 5 Prince Publishing

Cover Credit: Viola Estrella

First Edition 2018

5 PRINCE PUBLISHING AND BOOKS, LLC.

This book is dedicated to my delightful grandchildren.

FOREWORD

The year was 1971 and the time was like that hour between twilight and full dark, that time when anything is possible. That's how it was being young, I felt like the whole world was just waiting for me to blossom, to bloom, or to wither and fail. And while I was waiting for something huge to happen . . . life kept on rolling along in fits and starts, never slowing, always moving. Just like Stutter Creek, the one that meandered along beneath Crybaby Bridge.

he woods grew steadily thicker, the trees steadily taller. We went from traveling down a wide highway past brushy mesquite and stunted live oak to chugging down a narrow red-dirt road lined with huge cottonwoods, pines, and even something that looked and bloomed like dogwood. I wasn't positive about the species, though. Until now, I'd only ever seen it in books. In places, the trees actually met in a canopy overhead.

We had just crossed the border into New Mexico. I began to understand why it was called The Land of Enchantment. We didn't have foliage like this in West Texas. It amazed me. At home, I could name every plant and flower I could see. But here, just a few hours away, I'd arrived in a new world. It made me feel small and uneasy. It made me realize how insulated Crossroads, Texas really was.

"Isn't it great, Stevie-girl?" Jase, my best friend, sat beside me in the back seat. His dad was driving and his mom was riding shotgun. It had been a fairly quiet trip so far. I still couldn't believe they had invited me to go with them on their annual camping trip. I almost fell over when my Gramps said okay.

"It's beautiful." I smiled. "I can't get over how shady it is, even in the middle of the day." Did he know I'd never spent the night away from home, except with my previous best friend, Karla? But that was nothing like this. Before she moved off to California, Karla lived only a block from my house.

I gnawed at the cuticle around my thumb, trying not to let my nerves show. I was thirteen now. Not a little kid anymore. But I felt strange, self-conscious. I guess I just didn't want to embarrass myself in front of Jase's folks.

THE SUN HAD ALREADY slid past its apex when we pulled into the campsite. The clearing was at the very edge of Copper Lake. Tumbling out of the car, legs stiff from the long drive, we all stood staring at the vast stretch of water.

To me, it might as well have been the ocean. I couldn't even see the other shore.

"Level's way up," Mr. Lee said. "Had a lot of rain this year." He began unloading the trunk of the car.

I gazed out across the deep, calm water. With the sun on its downward trend, the surface of the lake appeared as solid as a sheet of beaten metal. I could see where it got its name.

"It's *huge*. Are we really going to hike around it?" The desire to hike the perimeter had been part of the conversation on the trip up.

Mr. Lee laughed and handed me the tent poles. "Don't worry, Stevie, we don't get too carried away. We just hike until we find a good spot to picnic or fish, then we stop for a swim. Usually, we never start up again . . ." His voice dropped off sharply and he turned half-away. "At least that's what we did when Rusty was here. He was always a lot more interested in swimming than in hiking or fishing."

Rusty is their older son. He went missing when his heli-copter was shot down in Vietnam last year. I wanted to pat Mr. Lee on the back or give him a hug the way I would do if it were Gramps or Jase who was hurting, but Mr. Lee was different. After they got the news about Rusty, he seemed to build a shell around himself. But it seemed like a brittle shell, one that might crack if we weren't careful with our words.

Mrs. Lee was almost as bad, except she didn't even have a shell, she just seemed fragile through and through. Like a very thin icicle, the kind you know will shatter when it falls.

I couldn't help but wonder if that was why they asked me along on the camping trip, to act as some sort of buffer. This would be their first trip since Rusty was listed as Missing in Action.

Even if that was the reason they invited me, I didn't mind. I spent a lot of time at their house. And Jase spent a lot of time at mine. It was eerie how different our families were.

At their house, it was always so quiet. At my house, even though it was just my Gramps and I, we always had noise of some kind. If we didn't have the TV or radio playing, then the two of us would be harmonizing on some old song.

I thought the other reason they asked me along was so that they couldn't change their minds and back out of going at the last second. That would have been the easy way out, just to not go at all. But it would also seem as if they'd given up on having a normal life.

Whatever the reason, I was thrilled. Not just because I had been invited, but thrilled that they were actually making an effort to include Jase in their lives again. Ever since Rusty went to Vietnam, Jase had been sort of like a ghost in his own home.

I caught a glimpse of movement from the corner of my eye.

"Think fast!"

I turned just in time to catch my rolled up sleeping bag from Jase.

Mr. and Mrs. Lee were clearing off space for our two tents, one for the girls and one for the guys. I had to stifle a laugh when Mrs. Lee actually brought out a broom—I was pretty sure I'd seen it in their barn—and started sweeping away small sticks and stones while Mr. Lee removed the larger twigs and branches from the area.

"C'mon, Stevie-girl," Jase said, eyeing his mom with a look of indulgence on his face. "Let's go find the firestones and firewood. When we get back, we'll help them finish setting up the tents."

I plopped my sleeping-bag-bedroll on the pile of supplies and followed Jase toward the woodland path.

"Not too far," Mr. Lee said. "We'll need those fire supplies before twilight. Besides, you know how quickly darkness falls in the woods..."

"Yes sir," Jase replied. "We're just going to check out Crybaby Bridge. Stevie can't wait to hear the baby." He chuckled as if it was our little joke.

I laughed, too. But with our shared history of attracting spirits and phantoms, I wasn't *really* certain I wanted to venture toward Crybaby Bridge. Not just yet, anyhow. Maybe tomorrow, in the bright light of morn.

There was no slowing Jase, though. He just kept strolling along, not even noticing how the tree shadows grew denser and darker the deeper we went. Silly boy. He was still under the mistaken impression that I was brave just because he'd seen me entering a haunted house one day.

"I can't believe we'll be in freshmen in a couple of months." My voice sounded loud in the woodsy silence. I laughed again to cover my nervousness.

Jase flipped his long hair off his forehead and smacked a mosquito against the side of his neck. "Me either."

I swatted at my own buzzing tormentor, which made me wonder just what it was that always caused mosquitos to get worse near sunset. Were they storing up food for overnight? Maybe I could research it when I got home. I loved researching things . . .

"I *said*, I can't wait to *finish* high school and get out of Crossroads." Jase had stopped walking and was waiting on me to catch up both physically and mentally.

"Sorry!" I ducked my head. He always caught me woolgathering, mulling things over, not paying attention. "But we haven't even *started* high school yet."

"True." His expression was thoughtful. "But after we do finish, we get to head off to college, where I can concentrate on writing stories and novels that people will read and talk about and still be reading long after I'm dead." He stopped abruptly, as if considering what he'd just said. "But before that, I might want to go out on the road like Jack Kerouac or Steinbeck and Charley . . ."

I know he didn't mean to break my heart when he looked so happy contemplating leaving me behind, but I just couldn't quite picture myself attending a big college. My Gramps had all those ambitions for me, but the thought of going off to school, to live in a dorm with a bunch of people I didn't know, literally made me nauseous.

Jase didn't notice my hesitation, though. He kept right on talking. "I just want to experience life. How can I write about it if I don't experience it? I might even want to be a war correspondent. You know, write a book about a day in the life of a soldier or something." His voice sounded taut, like a rubber band. I thought it might break if I pushed him to explain further.

Jase writing stories wasn't anything new. He'd recently written a short story about a girl who thought she was all alone when in reality she was surrounded by people who loved her.

He said the story was science fiction—he'd placed the girl on another planet surrounded by invisible beings that couldn't become visible until she acknowledged them.

I wondered if the story was about me, but I didn't have the nerve to ask. Loneliness wasn't something we talked about. But it did seem to be a recurring theme in our lives.

Late at night, I often recalled another story—the one that had cemented our friendship. It was a tale Jase had written about a small plane that crashed behind his house.

When the boy in the story had first encountered the ghost of the pilot standing beside his small, upside-down plane, the boy had asked if anyone else was inside.

"I was alone," the pilot had answered. "We all are."

Those words had chilled me, and yet, they also comforted me. I think it was because they absolved me of any need to go out and interact with people. I was a loner. I had my Gramps, I had Jase, and on the fringes, I had classmates Billy, Derol, and Karla (well, long distance, that is). The words of the pilot seemed to say that it doesn't matter if you have one friend or one hundred; in the end, we are all alone.

Maybe that's why I didn't quite share Jase's wanderlust. He was always more outgoing, more ready to experience new things. But when I said that to him once, he'd replied, "Shoot! I don't know why you say I'm outgoing. You're the one who went in the haunted house." Then he'd looked at me as if I were crazy. "You're the one who's brave, Stevie-girl. I just follow your lead."

Thinking about it later, I decided that I liked the way he saw me, even if it wasn't quite true.

Jase wasn't really what you'd call an extrovert. He didn't go and seek out other people's attention or approval, but maybe as a result of that, people sought him out. They respected him. He wasn't a jock. He said he only ran track because while he was running he could create whole new worlds in his head.

Sometimes, I would lie in my bed wondering just what it was that drew other kids to Jase. I'd first I'd thought it was his height, or his good looks, maybe even his kindness. But I didn't really think it was any of those, oh that may be why all the girls responded to him, but it didn't explain why even the other jocks —who couldn't care less about looks or kindness—seemed to respect him.

It was true, though.

I'd discovered this quality about Jase last year when Derol Pavey, a unique new student, came to our school and we wound up having to be his voice. That's when I first noticed that others literally stopped talking and listened when Jase spoke in class. And that awful night, when we had to hurry to the old abandoned school and look for Derol, almost the entire gym emptied as people left the dance and followed Jase.

I was convinced he had some inner something that others responded to. It will make him a great writer someday, I thought. It will take him far, far away from Crossroads, Texas. Far away from me.

I WAS STILL deep in thought when the lane ended and the creek appeared. It was wide, but it didn't look that deep, except maybe right in the middle. The bridge appeared quite ancient, its wide planks gray and warped. It sat atop thick support posts sunk down into the streambed. Along the edges, the water slipped and slurped and kicked along over the rocks and foliage lining the banks on either side.

"Guess I know why it's called Stutter Creek," I said, watching the current stop and start and meander along.

"Yeah, it does sort of stutter, doesn't it?" Jase replied.

We grinned at each other. We both knew we'd be back to

explore it more thoroughly after we'd finished setting set up camp.

I guess that's why he thought I was brave. I could never pass up a challenge, no matter how much it frightened me.

"C'mon." He took my hand. "We'd better get some wood and find some big stones for the fire pit." He glanced at the sky. Under the canopy of the forest, it was very dim.

I squeezed his fingers. I hoped nothing would ever come between us, but even as the thought crossed my mind, a chill wind tore across the bridge and flung dirt and leaf debris directly into our faces. We dropped hands and rubbed our eyes in disbelief.

Jase muttered, "What the heck was that?"

I rubbed my vision clear and gazed into the gathering gloom at the opposite end of the bridge. The wind whistled and whirled around our ankles like dusty water.

"I hope that doesn't mean a storm is coming," I said. What I really thought was, *something doesn't want us here.*

We started back toward the campsite. The way the crackly leaves were swirling, it was all I could do to see where to place my feet as I stumbled along behind Jase. When I ran my tongue across my teeth, I could feel the grit coating them. I closed my mouth and shielded my eyes.

"*Waahmaahhhh.*" The sound floated out of the dimness like a strand of spider silk flung onto the air.

I looked at Jase; he looked at me; and together, we ran.

After a bit, we realized the wind had died down to a gusty breeze. We slowed and began to grab up as many dry twigs and branches as our arms could hold.

"Did you hear it?" I asked.

Jase nodded. "It was the baby. The crybaby."

Clutching my armload of sticks, I entered the campsite. "Isn't this the same place your family always comes?"

He was right beside me. "Yep. But that's the first time I've ever heard *that* sound."

"Great," I muttered. "Guess it was just waiting for me."

2

*T*he camp was just as we'd left it. His parents had finished cleaning off the area. They had one tent set up and were working on the other.

Jase dropped his armload of braches and ran to help with the confusing jumble of strings, stakes, and poles. I dropped my own batch of sticks and twigs and began to search for the large stones for the fire ring. They weren't hard to find, apparently this was a popular place for campers. Either that, or these were the exact same stones the Lee family used every year. Each was about the size of a bowling ball, some larger and squarer, and all were black on one side. They weren't too far from the tents, just slightly scattered.

I gathered all the stones into a circle in what I hoped would be the appropriate place. It wasn't difficult to tell where the fires had been laid in previous campouts, not only were there two large logs placed in an L shape in the clearing, but when I swiped away the new carpet of dead leaves with my foot, the ground below was still a scorched-earth color. Just like the rocks.

"Good job, Stevie-girl," Mr. Lee said.

I didn't realize he was behind me until he spoke. "Thanks," I replied. "I hope this is the right place for the fire . . ."

"Perfect." His voice was kind. "I like the way you don't wait around for someone to tell you what to do. That's the mark of a true camper." He reached over and patted my shoulder curtly. For a moment, I thought he was going to tug the tip of my braid the way Jase always did.

THAT EVENING WE ATE HOTDOGS, which we stuck, lengthwise, onto sharpened sticks. I found out I loved sharpening my stick with Jase's pocketknife. After the dogs were charred and dripping into the fire, making the flames jump and hiss, we would place them carefully in the middle of the mustard-slathered bun waiting in our other palm. Then we would use the bun to pull the hotdog off the stick.

I only dropped mine once.

Potato chips, pickles, and relish completed our meal. For dessert we had already assembled all of our ingredients for s'mores: graham crackers, squares of a Hershey chocolate bar, and fat white marshmallows which we stuck right on the end of our hotdog sticks so that they, too, tasted faintly meaty when we ate them.

When the marshmallows were toasty, we slid them between the waiting chocolate-squares and crackers and pulled the gooey whiteness off the stick using the crackers much as we'd pulled the hotdog off using the bun.

The best part, besides actually eating them, was when someone's marshmallow would catch on fire and everyone would start blowing on it to put it out. I would always get the giggles. It was just so funny seeing Jase's normally taciturn parents laughing and blowing and acting like normal folks. I also liked it when we were roasting the hotdogs and grease would drip into the fire and sizzle and send up tiny sparks like fireflies.

It was very dark when we finished eating, and the fire was so pretty. The flames were orange, yellow, and blue beneath the blackened hardwood we'd gathered along the trail that afternoon.

Mr. Lee filled a bucket with sand and set it beside the fire. When it was time, the sand would smother the flames without soaking the wood. That way, we could reuse any unburned pieces for our breakfast fire.

It was kind of surreal to think that once upon a time, people had to build a fire every time they wanted to cook something. It was so easy to take things for granted—like turning on the stove with the simple twist of a knob.

Mr. Lee broke into my reverie by rubbing his palms together dramatically. "We'll have fish to fry tomorrow!" His eyes twinkled in the firelight.

I couldn't believe the difference in him out here. Mrs. Lee seemed different, too. As if they'd discarded their mantle of sadness back in Crossroads.

Mrs. Lee started putting away the condiments, and Jase and I were instructed to gather the hotdog/marshmallow sticks and feed them to the fire so the stickiness wouldn't attract ants or even bears.

"Are there *really* bears here?" I asked.

Jase grinned a wide, toothy grin and came creeping toward me with his hands hooked into claws above his head.

"Not funny!" I cringed away from him. "Go 'way, bear!"

Everyone laughed. Jase borrowed his dad's keys, went to the trunk of the car, and came back with a battered guitar. "I've been messing around with Rusty's old Harmony." His voice was carefully nonchalant.

He sat back down on the log and began to strum a tune. The

notes were so clear and unexpected on the cooling night air that an owl hooted above us, surprised by the song.

Jase played the opening bars of Janis Joplin's, "Me and Bobby McGee."

I was afraid he would ask me to sing, but he just looked at me in the waning firelight. Thank goodness, he didn't put me on the spot.

It was obvious he'd been practicing. He played the beginning of "Fortunate Son" by our favorite band, Creedence Clearwater Revival. Then he played most of "Galveston" by Glen Campbell. Both of those songs were about the war in Vietnam, and I knew he was playing them for Rusty just as surely as he'd played "Bobby McGee" for me.

After that, Jase strummed idly while the fire died down. Mr. Lee clasped him by the shoulder as he sat down beside him. "Sounds good, son," he said.

"Not as good as Rusty," Jase replied. "I'll never be that good, but I feel like I'm talking to him when I'm playing this old thing." He patted the guitar gently.

Mrs. Lee was conspicuously absent.

"It sounded great, to me, too." I smiled hesitantly.

Mr. Lee handed us each a flashlight, poured the bucket of sand on the fire, and ushered us off to our tents.

"And Stevie," he whispered as I passed him. "There aren't really any bears around here . . . haven't been in twenty years or more."

Behind him, Jase was holding the flashlight under his chin and making that awful toothy grin again.

I waited until Mr. Lee turned around, then I stuck my tongue out at Jase. When I turned to go in the tent to retrieve my toothbrush, Mrs. Lee was just coming out. She smiled sweetly. I think she saw me stick out my tongue. I felt silly, like a toddler with no manners.

After we traipsed down the short path to the public restrooms to get ready for bed, Mr. Lee checked the fire again; to make sure it was completely out. Then we all said goodnight and turned in.

I thought I would lie awake for hours, listening to Mrs. Lee's soft breathing in the darkness. It was a very odd feeling, sharing that tiny space with a woman I barely knew. But the moonlight was soft against the canvas of the tent. It made the fabric glow comfortingly around the seams and the tied-together door flap.

THE NEXT THING I KNEW, Mr. Lee was singing "Oh What a Beautiful Morning" at the top of his lungs. I heard Jase say something that caused them both to laugh, and then I heard the clang of pans knocking together. I imagined them jousting with frying pans.

I was surprised I'd slept so soundly. I didn't remember anything after noticing the glow of the moon. I'd slept straight through the night without a whimper. I guess all those things I'd heard about sleeping under the stars was right. It was the best sleep I'd ever had.

Mrs. Lee yawned and stretched. I sat up and rummaged through my suitcase for clean shorts.

"Morning," Mrs. Lee said. "Sounds like the guys are starting breakfast."

I nodded and smiled shyly. "Sounds to me like they're jousting . . ."

Mrs. Lee burst out laughing. "They probably are," she agreed. "C'mon." She grabbed her overnight bag. "Let's go down to the restroom and get dressed."

I pulled my flannel robe on over my pajamas and hoisted my own overnight case. I'd wondered how we would handle getting dressed in front of each other; I guess she'd been wondering the same thing.

"Ah, there's my sunshine," Mr. Lee exclaimed when he saw his wife. Then he began to sing, "You Are My Sunshine."

I couldn't help laughing. When I glanced at Jase, he was grinning. The whole family seemed to have broken through the agony of Rusty's disappearance like sunshine breaking through rainclouds.

We dressed quickly. Mrs. Lee suggested I wear my swimsuit under my shorts because we would probably end up swimming later in the day.

When we returned to camp, I was glad to see that Jase and I had gathered enough firewood the evening before, and with the pieces left over from the previous fire, we were all prepared for breakfast this morning.

The campsites were situated at the far end of the Burl River, which wound its way lazily through the Sacramento Mountains where the little town of Stutter Creek was located. This particular campsite was right on the banks of Copper Lake, with a dusty red beach on one side, and thick brush on the other. Stutter Creek was a tributary of the Burl, which rushed over the dam and emptied right into the lake. It was a gorgeous area. Gazing around, I could feel my spirit expanding to fill the large, green space. In West Texas, water was a luxury. Here, I felt rich beyond compare.

Mr. Lee said if we weren't too loud, we might catch a glimpse of the abundant deer that moved through the brush like careful shadows.

Together, we cooked a huge breakfast of bacon, eggs, and fried toast. It was delicious. I learned the truth about something else I'd always heard: food does taste better outdoors, cooked over an open fire.

But even as I was enjoying the breakfast, I was worrying

about my Gramps back home. He was my only family except for my long-lost father who had gone out for cigarettes one evening and never returned. I think he'd been arguing with my mom at the time.

When he didn't return after a few weeks—and money became as scarce as water—my mom moved us to Crossroads to live with Gran and Gramps. My father had visited us there once, for Christmas, and then he'd gotten a call from someone, and he was gone again.

Mom finally went in search of him. She'd heard he was in Amarillo. But on the way there, an 18-wheeler had run a stop sign and crashed into her car. The truck had been carrying a load of feed for the dairy farms in that area. Gramps said Mom never knew what hit her. Later, I decided that was a good thing. It meant she didn't suffer.

Gran passed on a few years later. She had a stroke. Guess that's why I worried so about my Gramps. He was pretty much all I had in the whole world.

I wondered what he was having for breakfast. We usually cooked together on Saturday, if he didn't have to work at the Police Department where he was a dispatcher. Maybe he'd gone down to The Bluebird Café and had breakfast with Mr. Pearcy. I hoped he had. I didn't like to think of him eating alone.

THE DAY WHIPPED past in a hurry. We explored the banks of the lake, and hiked around the perimeter until we found a good fishing hole—and vowed to come back and fish later—and then we stripped off our shirts and shorts and jumped in the water.

For lunch, we had bologna sandwiches and sliced tomatoes. Lays potato chips never tasted so good. We washed it all down with our thermos's of iced tea—which was a little melted but still very refreshing in the heat of the day.

It was a wonderful picnic, and before we knew it, Mr. and Mrs. Lee were telling us it was time to get out and head to the showers to clean up before supper.

Imagine our dismay when we got to the public restrooms and found that they were closed for repair. Apparently, there had been a leak while we were out swimming. All that was available were a couple of Port-a-Potties—no showers whatsoever.

It didn't really bother me. After swimming, I didn't feel that dirty, except my hair was kind of lank. But Mrs. Lee said she was certain she smelled like a fish.

I laughed and assured her she didn't.

We set up the badminton net and played for over an hour. First it was girls against the boys, but after a while, we switched and played parents against kids. I don't think I ever laughed so hard in my life. Sometimes, when I hit the little plastic birdie, it would bounce off my racket and go straight up. Jase would chase it and try to help it on over the net, but often, he was laughing as hard as me. It was just so funny to run around gazing straight up at the sky, waiting for the little thing to fall onto our rackets.

Once, I was almost certain I heard something on the wind, and I was reminded of the Jimi Hendrix song, "The Wind Cried Mary." But when I stopped and listened closely, I didn't hear anything at all.

Finally, we all grew hungry again. All that exercise I suppose. Since we hadn't gone fishing yet, we had another sandwich, pimiento cheese this time, and it could not have tasted any better.

Mrs. Lee surprised us when she pulled out a foil-wrapped pan of chewy fudge brownies. We even had individual pints of milk in the ice chest to go with them. "We will pick up more milk when we go to the camp store," she said.

I felt as if I had gone straight to Heaven. Although I was always happy at home with my Gramps, this was a new kind of joy. Playing and swimming, picnicking and listening to music around the campfire—even as it was happening, I knew these were going to be some of the best memories of my life.

After our sandwiches there wasn't much to clean up, so Jase and I decided, on the spur of the moment, to stroll down and check out the bridge again. I was a bit leery. If we ran into another isolated dust storm, I was prepared to tell Jase I was never going back.

We walked slowly. It wasn't far, and as we dawdled on the lane, Jase pointed out several examples of poison oak and poison ivy. We even tried to identify the songs of birds. The mockingbird was the most prevalent, its clear voice carried through the woods like a beacon.

I think we may have been consciously trying to delay arriving at the bridge. I'm not certain, but if so it worked. Twilight was upon us when we finally arrived.

Even though I had teased Jase when he grabbed the flashlight as we left camp, I was glad now. It also meant we could only stay a minute, and then we had to head right back. I was sort of glad about that, too. Even though I told myself that I *wanted* to investigate the infamous Crybaby Bridge, I didn't want to find out too much. At this point, I wasn't sure whether I wanted the tale about the crying baby to be real, or whether I'd be more relieved to find out that the whole thing was just an urban legend.

"THERE IT IS." Jase's voice held a note of awe.

The bridge was ghostly in the last light of day. The far end was shrouded in woodsy darkness and the sound of the creek lapping at the thick support posts was very clear in the quiet early eve.

We stepped onto the bridge cautiously, gauging the strength

of the slats with each careful step. When we got to the middle, we stood side-by-side looking down over the railing, watching the path of the waning light on the crinkly water as it bounced over the rocks. A cool breeze tickled our arms. A night bird called in the distance, and the smell of the clear-running creek reminded me of spring rain.

"Do you think that was really a baby crying?" I murmured.

Jase shrugged. "I figure there's probably just a loon nearby or something. I've heard people say loons can sound like a person crying."

I shivered and moved closer to his tall form. "I hope we don't —""*Waahhhmaahhh.*" The sound whispered toward us like an invisible firework.

I clutched Jase's arm and craned my head around to try and spot the loon. I'd discovered that the older I got, the less I like to be frightened. I think our encounters with the supernatural back in Crossroads were killing off my bravery cells the same way the TV ads said drugs will kill off your brain cells.

"Waahhh—"

I smashed myself against Jase. "It's the same thing we heard before . . . is that what a loon sounds like?" All the sounds were similar, but the last one sounded as if it had been abruptly cut off.

"I don't know," he admitted. "I never heard a loon before."

His arm muscles were tense. It felt as if I were clutching the strings of a harp. I held on even tighter. I could almost see the air thrumming along with our nerves. My eyes strained to see into the gathering darkness across the creek, or down at the other end of the bridge.

"Waahhhmaahh . . ."

"That's no loon." I pointed to a shimmery figure standing on the opposite bank below us.

"It looks like a woman." Jase murmured. "What's she wearing, a nightgown?"

The fabric did appear to be quite thin, or perhaps that was because of the rays of fading light behind her. "What's she *doing*?"

Jase shook his head. "She appears to be looking for something . . ."

My breath froze in my throat.

She was coming toward us, toward the bridge. Her eyes were downcast, searching the banks of the creek as she glided along.

"*Waahhhmaaahh.*" The sound was louder.

My skin crawled. "Was that her?"

Jase shook his head again.

Suddenly, I caught a glimpse of movement beneath us as something pink floated out from under the bridge.

"It's a baby," I shouted. "In the water!" I yanked Jase's arm and pointed at the swirling, stuttering creek.

The woman dove in and disappeared. All that was left was a shimmer of white beneath the skin of the creek and a lazy splotch of long dark hair that floated outward around her head in a soft caul.

The baby spun and eddied with the current. A bit further down, it came to rest in a tangle of twigs and branches jutting out from the bank.

Jase was off the bridge and onto the shore in nothing flat.

I was right behind him.

The infant was face down in the mud and the muck at the edge of the water.

It was clad in nothing but a dingy diaper.

"Ohhhh," my voice quavered as Jase reached for the chubby little arm to turn the baby over. One of its eyes was gone and the other stared sightlessly from beneath stiff black lashes. The rough blonde hair was plastered flat.

"It's a doll!" Jase yanked the thing from the muddy bank in disgust. It made a slight sucking sound as the mire relinquished its grip. Now I could see that the diaper was simply painted on. The pink color of the plastic showed through in several places.

"*Waahhmaahhh!*" The awful sound came from the little pattern of speaker holes in the doll's chest.

Jase dropped it on the ground and wiped his hands on his shirt. "Who would do such a horrible thing?"

We heard a snicker behind us. It was so low I couldn't tell if it was male or female. But it made me furious and I started toward the sound without thinking. I could hear Jase behind me. In a second, he was even with me, then past me. That's when I realized I could see the circle of his flashlight bobbing ahead of me.

All at once, I heard a muffled, "Oomph!"

"Jase?" I called. "You okay?"

"Yeah, c'mon, Stevie-girl. I think I found the owner of our little one-eyed dolly."

I hurried toward the sound of his voice, and there they were. Jase's thick blond hair gleamed in the darkness of the trail. It was almost as bright as the long blonde hair of the girl on the ground.

"Who are you?" I stood aside as she got to her feet.

Jase shined the flashlight on her sullen face. She had tripped over a jumble of tree roots jutting up from the ground.

"Nora." Her voice matched her expression. "I live near the camp store." Jase kept the light on her face. "You mean that place where you buy live bait?"

Nora nodded, dusting at the leaf rubbish stuck to her knees, ignoring the beam illuminating her like a spotlight.

"Why were you spying on us? Did you put that doll in the water?" I tried to keep the tremor from my voice, but I was getting angrier by the minute. *What an ugly trick that had been.*

To my amazement, tears began to seep from Nora's eyes as if

she'd sprung a leak. "It was just an old baby doll," her voice was defensive. "Nothing to get so riled up about." She peered around us.

Jase and I looked at each other in the gloom. *What is she looking for?*

"How many times have you done this to people?" he asked.

Nora tilted her head back and stuck out her bottom lip. She looked like a two year old in a teenager's body. "It's nothing," she said. "Don't be so *righteous* for crying out loud." She swiped angry tears off her cheeks, pushed past us, and went back toward the bridge.

We had little choice but to follow.

Imagine our amazement when she walked right past the old doll and headed off in the direction of the camp store.

"Unbelievable," Jase muttered. "Un-be-*liev*-able!" He kicked a rock. "And she didn't even take the doll."

I glanced toward it. The thing looked pitiful lying there in the muck. "We'd better get it." I didn't want to touch it. But I had to. The plastic was cold, slightly slimy from the vegetation at the water's edge. "Just doesn't seem right to leave it there for someone else to find." I held it gingerly, by the hard plastic fingers.

"Waahh*maahh!*"

I couldn't help myself. I dropped it, too.

"*Waahm*—" Its voice cut off suddenly.

I covered my ears with my hands.

Jase grimaced and picked it up. "Can't believe this," he said. "I have to show it to my folks." He glanced back toward the creek. "Sure wouldn't want them to be tricked like that." He carried it back to camp cradled in his arms as if it were a real baby. That was the only way to keep it from crying out.

We walked in silence.

Neither of us mentioned the lady in white. I think we both

knew she was a phantom. Even if the crying *baby* was a hoax, we knew what we'd seen when the woman dove into the water. It was just too much like the phantom pilot in Jase's backyard, and the phantom student who had mysteriously appeared in my bathroom mirror after the arrival of Derol Pavey at our school last year.

I wondered if we had somehow become phantom magnets.

WHEN JASE SPILLED the details of Nora and the doll, Mr. and Mrs. Lee were amazed.

"Well, I guess Miss Nora wants to make sure the tourists get their money's worth at Crybaby Bridge." Mr. Lee shook his head.

Mrs. Lee looked at him. "We'll have to tell her parents." A shadow crossed her face. "She can't be allowed to keep doing this. What if someone tried to jump in and save the thing and ... what if they drowned?" She glanced at the doll—still cradled in Jase's arms—and shuddered.

"Yes, I suppose you're right," her husband agreed. "We'll make it a point to seek them out the next time we go to the store."

Jase looked from me, to his mom, then to his dad. "What should I do with this?" He held the baby slightly forward, still being so careful not to tilt it in such a way that it would make that dreadful sound.

Mr. Lee looked around the campsite. "In our tent?"

Jase shook his head, a look of distaste on his face.

"Don't look at me," I said, backing away. "No way I could sleep with it in *our* tent."

"Me either," Mrs. Lee agreed. "How about the trunk of the car?"

We all approved of that idea, and I ducked inside the "girls" tent and came back out with an old tee shirt I'd brought to wear over my swimsuit. "Wrap her in this." I handed the shirt to Jase.

Everyone looked at me.

"It just doesn't seem right to leave her with nothing on but a diaper." I realized I had begun to refer to the doll as "she," but I couldn't seem to stop myself.

Jase took my shirt and draped it around the doll like a blanket. Mr. Lee opened the trunk with his key and Jase laid he doll inside, out of sight.

I didn't know why it bothered me when Mr. Lee closed the lid. It's only a doll, I kept telling myself. But deep down, I was terrified we were still going to hear her cry, and then what would we do? The thought of opening the trunk back up to a find a crying child wriggling inside my old shirt was almost more than I could bear.

3

That night we were all a bit more subdued that the night before. We ate our hotdogs again, and we all laughed and joked, but it felt forced.

We went to bed after Jase played a few more songs on Rusty's guitar. For some reason, it just wasn't the same. The joy seemed to have leaked out of the day. Maybe we had locked it in the trunk of the car with the doll.

With any luck, it will be better tomorrow, I thought. I crossed my fingers in hopes of making it so.

Sometime during the night, I awoke to the sound of Mrs. Lee crying almost soundlessly in the darkness. I couldn't tell if she was awake or asleep, so I didn't say anything. I just pulled my sleeping bag up over my head and pretended I was asleep.

I figured she was probably missing Rusty, and that she'd been putting on a brave front up until now. It had to be difficult, being in their family vacation place without him. I recalled how awful it had been when the military chaplain had brought the news that he was missing in action. I'd thought Mrs. Lee would never get out of her bed again, but she did. I guess she was stronger than she appeared.

The next morning, she looked none the worse for wear, so I didn't say anything. What would I have said, anyway? I'm just a kid. Who knows, maybe I was only dreaming.

We had French toast for breakfast, with strips of crisp bacon, and then we cleaned up our breakfast dishes, washing them in a big bucket of boiled lake water.

After we were all dressed in our suits and shorts again, we hiked up around the creek, all the way to the place where it widened out in preparation for joining the river. After a few hours of hiking and playing in the water, we wound up at the little store.

Nora was nowhere to be seen, but Mr. Lee asked the store-owner if he knew her. He claimed that no one fitting that description lived nearby.

Mr. Lee thanked him and said perhaps we were mistaken.

He did say there was a new housing development on the other side of the lake and that perhaps that's where she lived.

Jase looked at me with a bland expression on his face. I knew that meant he didn't want me to say anything. We both knew what we'd heard. By now, we were old hands at keeping things to ourselves, and at figuring those things out when they didn't seem to be as they appeared.

Jase and Mr. Lee ventured over to the large bait tank on the opposite side of the store and watched as the proprietor scooped live minnows into an old Folger's coffee can. He handed the red can to me to carry. It was half-filled with water and I tried not to slosh it over the edge. The man handed me a plastic lid with holes punched in it. I fitted the lid down over the lip of the metal can and walked outside to wait.

I really didn't want to stick a live minnow on my fishhook. I did not like to think about that horrible hook stabbed into the tiny fish. Gramps always said they didn't feel things like we did, but still . . . I couldn't stand seeing them flop about on the end of the line, or on the bank, gasping for air. I just really didn't like fishing very much at all. I did like to *eat* fried fish, though. And I loved sitting on the bank in the shade, watching the bobber dance about in the sunlight. Guess that's always the way in life, good with the bad. That's how it seemed anyhow. But I still didn't think I could stick that hook in.

Jase and his dad came out carrying a paper sack with tubular bags of Lay's salted peanuts and four bottles of cold Dr. Pepper. My eyes lit up. I loved dumping peanuts into a bottle of Dr. Pepper and watching it foam, then drinking the salty mixture, tapping the bottom of the bottle to get all the softened nuts.

Grinning, Jase took the bait can from me and carried it the rest of the way. When we were almost out of the parking lot, I got the sensation that someone was watching us. I don't know why, but it was as if the flesh on the back of my neck was suddenly exposed, sort of itchy. I scratched at it just in case an insect was crawling, but something also made me turn around and look behind us, and there was Nora.

She was standing at the far corner of the little white clapboard store peering at us as we walked away. Just as I was about to say something, she ducked backward and was gone.

"What is it?" Jase asked.

I hesitated another second, to be certain she was gone. "It was Nora. She was peeking around the corner at us."

Jase and his dad glanced back at the store. "Probably afraid we were going to tell someone what she did last night."

"Odd," Mr. Lee said. "The store owner just got through saying that no little girl like that lived around here—now why would he say that?" His brow wrinkled as he spoke. Then he turned around and looked back at the store. I liked the way he lumped himself in there with us, so we'd know he was on our side.

He adjusted his fishing hat on his head, careful not to poke his fingers on any of the colorful lures pinned around the band. "Every time I think about how that doll must have looked under the bridge, I get a little angrier."

We didn't say anything. I don't know about Jase, but I didn't really want Nora to get in trouble. I sure didn't like the thought of her pulling that prank on other people, though. Especially someone like Mrs. Lee who was already grieving.

Walking down the red dirt road with our minnows and our snacks, I began to feel the heat on the top of my head and on my collarbones. I'd worn my favorite red tank top and blue jean cutoffs. My hair was braided, as usual, to keep it off out of my face, but I was still beginning to get sweaty and sticky. This close to the lake, the humidity in the air clung to my skin like a damp cloth. Mosquitos and tiny flies began to bump and buzz around my head. I noticed Jase waving at his own face every now and then, too.

"Need a little rain shower," Mrs. Lee said. "Clean the air of these bothersome bugs."

"After we catch our supper, maybe we can go swimming again. That'll help." Jase smacked something on the side of his neck as he spoke.

I nodded. If they had asked me I would've said skip the fishing and just go swimming. We could always roast another hot dog for supper.

But they didn't ask, and in moments we were nearing the bridge. This time we were coming at it from the opposite direction. We hadn't mentioned the woman we thought we'd seen the night before, but nevertheless, my eyes scanned the muddy bank for any telltale footprints. There were none.

We crossed over without incident.

Mrs. Lee led us all back into camp. While the guys gathered our fishing poles, I helped her put together another little picnic in the ice chest. She also grabbed a large canvas tote bag that I hadn't noticed before.

When we were ready, Jase grinned and gave his mom a hug. I hadn't seen him do that since the night the military men came and told them Rusty was MIA. That night, he'd lain beside his mom on his parent's big bed, and I had covered the two of them with a quilt. His dad had been out of town. In a reverse way, it had reminded me of the night my own mom had been killed.

Gramps had lain beside me on my little bed. We hadn't said anything; he had simply patted my back and told me everything would be all right. He was still there when I awoke the next morning. After the funeral, I told him he didn't have to sleep with me anymore. Gran was still alive, then. I think she was glad when I told Gramps I would be all right. She had looked so small in their high, feather bed all by herself. A few years later, she was gone, too. A stroke. Sudden and unexpected.

WE TOOK the lunch Mrs. Lee had prepared, and the fishing poles and bait, then we started around the edge of the lake until we arrived at the "fishing hole" we'd found the day before. I got the idea that this was pretty much the same place they fished every year.

Jase's face was pink from the sun. His green eyes scanned the bank eagerly. When he found the exact spot he was looking for, he set the tackle box down and popped the lid off the Folger's can before setting it aside, too.

Without asking, he took the end of my fishing line and tied a hook onto it. I looked away when he placed the minnow on the hook. Then he did the same for his line. Further down the bank, his dad was baiting Mrs. Lee's hook.

The lake was smooth and sparkly. But now, the overhead sun reflected off it as if it were a giant sheet of slightly-used tinfoil rather than a sheet of beaten copper as it had appeared in the rays of the setting sun. Seeing this, I was surprised when it was cold as we waded out away from the bank. As hot as the day was becoming, I'd thought the water would be warm.

"Later in the summer, it will get warmer," Mrs. Lee said, seeing the look on my face as my bare ankles met the chilly water.

We flung our hooks into the water, making certain to stand a good distance apart from one another (I don't think they trusted me), and then we slowly dragged them back to shore hoping that our wriggling minnows would attract some hungry fish.

When I pulled my hook out of the water, there was no wriggling minnow. I wasn't sure what had happened. But I didn't tell anyone. I just flipped it back out into the water and pretended it was still there.

After a few moments, Jase jerked his line. "I've got a bite!"

"Careful," his dad said. "Set the hook, don't let him get away . . ."

I could see a silvery slice of something split the skin of the water every few seconds as it fought the hook, but I didn't enjoy it the way the guys did. I didn't like watching something fight for its life, especially knowing we were going to kill it and eat it. And yet, I felt silly for being that way. The life or death struggle didn't bother anyone else, not even Mrs. Lee; in fact, she ran and grabbed the short-handled net so that she would be ready to scoop the fish out of the water as soon as Jase got it close to shore.

"Atta boy," Mr. Lee said as Jase played out a bit of line and then reeled it back. "Tire him out, no, no, don't give him too much, he'll take your bait . . ."

I stood there, my line flat on the surface of the water, watching and trying to enjoy, and then I got that feeling on the back of my neck again. As if my skin was wrinkling up like crepe paper.

Slowly, I turned.

The woman in white was standing just inside the tree line behind us. Her gown glowed even in the full daylight and I wanted to look away. Except I couldn't. The fabric of her attire looked wet, as if she'd just walked out of the water, but of course she hadn't. Not here anyway. We would've seen her. It wasn't a nightgown though; this close I could see that. It looked sort of like a nurse's uniform. White cotton fabric. Thin. Almost transparent.

I tried smiling at her the way I had smiled at the little phantom student who used to appear in my bathroom mirror, but if this phantom lady could see my smile, she didn't acknowledge it. Instead, she simply stared at me, and at Mrs. Lee as she slipped the net into the water below the flickering fish.

When I looked back, she was gone.

After catching three good-sized perch—two for Jase, and one for his dad—his mom and I started back to camp. The guys were going to stay at the creek and clean the fish. Mr. Lee didn't want to clean the fish near our camp. He said it might attract varmints.

I didn't mind a bit. Cleaning fish was one of those skills I didn't care if I *never* learned. Besides, his mom was going to show me how to get the seasoning ready. She called it the fish fry. As we walked, she told me the ingredients. Mostly, it consisted of cornmeal, flour, salt, black pepper, cayenne pepper, and a hearty dash of paprika.

When the guys got back with the fish, neatly skinned and fileted, we dropped the damp strips into the brown paper bag of seasoning to coat them. From there, they went into the hot iron skillet coated with a big white lump of Crisco lard. In another skillet, we'd already fried up a couple of potatoes with onions.

The smell was out of this world. If there are any bears, I thought, this wonderful scent is certain to bring them on the *run*.

My stomach began to growl.

It was a *feast*. In addition to the fish and potatoes, we also had sliced tomatoes and corn fritters that Mrs. Lee made in a Dutch oven.

After another quick cleanup, Jase and I shucked our shorts and raced each other to the lake for a swim.

It was late afternoon and the strong sun had finally warmed the surface of the water to bath temperature. Away from the shallows, however, the deeper water was still cold.

"I see why fish are cold blooded." I squealed as an icy current caressed my legs.

"Don't go out too far." Mrs. Lee's face was a mask of concern.

"We won't, Mom . . ." Jase jerked his head toward me and we both swam closer to shore. Neither of us wanted to give her anything else to worry about.

Just as I was warming up again, Jase grabbed my ankle and pulled me under.

I came up spluttering and splashed him as hard as I could. He just laughed and swam out of reach.

I tried to get revenge, but I couldn't catch him.

All of a sudden, Mr. Lee was there. He was a big man. He grabbed Jase like a little boy and threw him into the air. This time, Jase came up spluttering. I laughed so hard I thought I would burst.

Mr. Lee swam away from Jase just as Jase had swum away from me.

We heard a tiny splash and Mrs. Lee was throwing floatie things into the water. That must've been what she had in the tote bag. I couldn't believe she'd blown them all up for us.

I grabbed a black inner tube and heaved myself onto it by popping up through the middle and floundering about until I was finally laid out across it. My arms were dangling over the sides, my head was back, and my legs were stuck over the other side. My bottom was down in the hole, in the water.

I sighed, prepared to relax and catch a few rays.

Jase threw a beach ball at my head and I flipped over backward trying to avoid it. "You've had it now, boy!" I cried, when I surfaced.

He grabbed my inner tube and went swimming away.

Once again, Mr. Lee came to my rescue. He dove under the water and Jase went down. Mr. Lee had swept his feet right out from under him. He tossed me my inner tube and I managed to get on it again.

Mrs. Lee waded out into the shallows and lay down on a flat, inflatable mattress. "I'm not blowing up anything else!" she declared. Her face was flushed. It was almost the same shade as my red tank top.

We floated around for a few minutes while Jase did his best to dunk his dad. But that wasn't happening. Mr. Lee was an excellent swimmer. Mrs. Lee said he had several swimming trophies from his college days. I wondered why I'd never seen them—I'd been a frequent visitor to their home—but then I recalled how Jase said his parents didn't believe in self-promotion. It was sort of against their religion.

At last, Mr. Lee allowed Jase to catch him and pull him down into the water. He came up grinning and headed to shore. The sun was getting low and the currents tickling my legs were becoming downright icy again.

"Few more minutes," he called. "I'm going down to the showers, when I get back, it's time to get out."

"I'll come with you," Mrs. Lee said. "I don't really want to be down there alone. That place sort of gives me the willies." She dragged her floatie mattress onto the bank to dry.

They walked down the lane, hand in hand, and I thought perhaps they'd gotten back on track after the melancholy night we'd had last night. Even as the thought crossed my mind, an image of Rusty popped up, unbidden. I turned to find Jase staring at me, as if he'd seen my thoughts.

"You ready to get out," he asked.

"Almost—oh my!" I gasped and pointed toward the opposite bank.

Jase turned quickly and I leaped on his back and was finally able to topple him. I held him under as long as humanly possible before he tossed me aside and surfaced as easily as Poseidon, God of the Deep.

"Now I'm ready to get out," I yelled, dashing for shore.

He almost caught me when I stopped to snag the inner tube, but at the last second, he stumbled and I was able to make it all the way back to the tents.

"You got lucky that time, Stevie-girl," he cried. "But revenge is sweet! Just remember that when you find a creepy-crawly in your sleeping bag tonight."

I cringed, but I would never let on that I was worried. "Ha!" I replied. "I'd come nearer to picking up a creepy-crawly before you would. Remember that poor tarantula that almost frightened you into an early grave? And he was just crawling across the yard . . . maybe you'd better check *your* sleeping bag tonight!" I giggled loudly to let him know I wasn't scared.

He grabbed the canvas door of my tent and gave it a hearty shake as he walked by.

I almost fainted.

---

he sun was drowning in the lake behind us when Jase and I walked back down to the bridge, to see if our episode from the night before would be repeated. We had our clean clothes under our arms. Our intention was to check it out, and then double back to the showers.

"I'm glad we didn't see or hear anything when we crossed the bridge with your folks earlier."

"Me, too," Jase agreed. "Although I can't help but wonder why other people don't see the things we do . . ."

I nodded. I was glad I wasn't the only one who wondered about that.

The little slice of sun that was still visible above the horizon behind us was now almost completely blocked by the thick trees. That meant the bridge was already bathed in shadows. We approached it cautiously, expecting to see the woman or hear the baby, or both. Of course, now that we knew Nora was behind the "crying" baby doll, we weren't really afraid of that happening again.

There was one thing that still bothered me about that, though. According to legend, the crying had been heard for decades, not just since a blonde girl with a bad attitude had moved in nearby.

"I wonder how long Nora has lived here?" The water beneath the bridge was brown, as if the mud along the bank had been stirred up recently. I leaned against the railing and peered into the murky depths.

Jase leaned over the opposite rail. "I don't think she said. Why?"

I walked to his side of the bridge. The wooden planks were old and rough. I was glad I was wearing my Keds. Long gray splinters jutted up here and there. "I just wondered. I mean, if it was Nora and the baby doll making that awful crying sound . . ." I hesitated, half-expecting to hear it on cue. The woods were quiet. Only the stuttering water broke the silence.

"Then what was making it all the other years, before Nora came?" Jase finished my thought, as usual.

"Loons," we said together.

We automatically hooked pinky fingers. "You owe me—"

"—a Coke," he finished.

"Hurry up, kids!" Mr. Lee called from the trail. "It'll be full dark soon . . ."

"Coming, Dad." Jase turned and headed toward the bathrooms.

I hurried to keep up, but I couldn't help looking over my shoulder as we left the bridge.

Thank goodness, there was nothing there.

Nothing at all.

"DID you see her at the fishing hole," I asked as we walked the short distance to the restrooms.

"Who, Nora?"

"The woman in white," I replied.

Jase shook his head. "Was she in the water, like before?"

"No, she was standing behind us, watching." I rubbed at the sudden gooseflesh coating my arms. "It gave me the creeps."

"I'll bet." He pawed the shock of hair off his forehead. "Was she still wearing that night gown?"

"It looked the same, but I don't think it's a nightgown after all. I'm pretty sure it's some kind of uniform." I scuffed the toe of my shoe in the fine dust of the trail. "It was solid white, like those uniforms nurses wear."

"It's getting to the point where I almost *expect* to see these ethereal creatures when I'm with you." He grinned to take the sting out his words. Then he looped an arm about my shoulders and pulled me, briefly, to his side.

"We're going on back to camp," Mrs. Lee said as we approached. "The showers aren't bad at all now that they've got the leak repaired." She smiled. "Just make it quick because the hot water doesn't last very long."

"We will," Jase replied. "It won't take but a minute for me to wash the lake off."

I laughed nervously. "It might take me a couple of minutes to wash my hair." I wondered if I could get away with just rinsing it, but I knew I wouldn't do that. Mrs. Lee had convinced me that since the lake smelled like fish, we probably did, too.

I made Jase promise to stand guard outside the Women's side of the rest room until I was done. Inside, the shower was simply an open space blocked off from the rest of the bathroom with a three-quarter-height wall tiled in the same beige as the rest of the room. There was no door at all. It smelled surprisingly clean, like Clorox bleach, and I soon found out why. In each toilet— there were three stalls, with doors—was a cake of bowl cleaner clamped onto the rim with a wire fastener.

I began to feel a little better. The room was brightly lit, and I could see every inch of it. There was no place for anyone to hide.

The doors to every stall hung open, and there was a long tiled bench along one wall. High up, right under the ceiling, a row of frosted windows looked out on the place where Jase was standing guard. Of course the windows were simply for ventilation. One would have to be ten feet tall to see out—or in.

I placed my clothes on the bench and hung my towel and washcloth over the partial wall so that it would be available to me when I was in the shower.

"It's okay . . ." I opened the door to the outside, and stuck my head through the gap. "I'm the only one here." I started to pull my head back inside. "You won't let anyone come in while I'm in there, will you?"

He shook his head and watched as I unbraided my hair. Although he loved to play pranks on me in the lake, I knew I could trust him not to prank me while I was in the shower. Jase was my best friend. I trusted him more than anyone. Except my Gramps.

Satisfied no one would get past my personal bodyguard, I closed the door and crossed the open space to the tiled bench. It was about knee high, sort of an extension of the wall. I slipped off my Keds and stepped into the shower to turn the water on and warm it up to the right temperature. Then I slipped out of my clothes and lathered up quickly.

Mrs. Lee was right. I'd barely got the shampoo rinsed out of my hair when the hot water began to run out. First it became tepid, then cool, and in moments it was downright cold.

Shivering, I reached to turn off the handle.

That's when I saw the shadow.

One of the stall doors was swinging closed in slow motion. I could see the slim gray shadow of the metal door creeping stealthily across the cement floor like the arm of a sundial.

My hand froze. The water went from cold to icy. My skin began to sting where the water was striking it.

I wanted to yell for Jase. Where was he? How did someone get past him? Wait . . . if I could see the shadow of the stall door, why couldn't I see the shadow of the person pulling the door closed?

Without turning off the water, thinking the sound of it would somehow mask the sound of my movements; I slid my towel off the tiled divider and wrapped it securely around my body. My wet hair was cold where it lay against my neck and shoulders.

Trying to make *myself* into a shadow, I took a deep, quiet, breath to calm my nerves. Clutching my towel securely, I peered around the edge of the tiled half-wall.

The door to the first stall was completely closed. It was either locked from the inside, or someone was holding it shut. The doors to the other two stalls were still gaping open just like they had been when I came in.

Would Jase do that? To scare me?

Of course not. Why was I even thinking such a thing?

I leaned over to see if there were any feet visible under the stall door—neither the door nor the walls went all the way to the floor. It was the typical gray metal stall.

As I was bent over, trying to see under the door, something white slipped beneath the side wall and into the *middle* stall.

Left in its place was a puddle of fishy smelling water.

The woman in white?

I didn't have time to find out.

The middle door slammed shut with an ear splitting bang of metal on metal.

The third door, the one on the end of the row, followed suit. Soon, all three doors were flapping back and forth like the wings of great metal birds.

I shrieked and dashed to the bench, grabbed my clothes, and headed for the outer door just as the third stall door *crashed* open and hit the wall hard enough to chip the tile. The tiny piece of glazed ceramic flew past me and landed near the central floor drain.

Jase flung open the big door. His eyes were wild. "Stevie! What is it?"

I rushed past him and into the night wearing nothing but a towel, clutching my shoes and clothes to my chest.

Behind me, I could hear the cacophony of doors still clapping.

Suddenly, all was still. The only sound was the ringing echo of the metal door that had struck the tile wall.

Jase backed out of the open door.

"Don't look!" I warned as I hurriedly pulled on my clean clothes.

"What was it?" he demanded. "Was it the woman?"

"I think so." I zipped my jeans and stepped into my Keds. I didn't even care that I'd just stuck my damp and dirty feet into my shoes. I'd run out of the bathroom barefooted, right into the fine red dirt.

Jase stood still, listening. All we could hear was the sound of the shower. I'd left it running full blast.

We looked at each other in the automatic outdoor light that had just winked on in the darkness.

"Jase!" I pointed to the frosted window under the bathroom's overhang.

He whirled around.

There was a face pressed to the inside of the window. Since the glass was frosted, it was difficult to discern facial features, but I was certain it was the woman in white. I could see a dark nimbus of hair framing the face.

Jase yanked open the door—again—and we both rushed inside.

The spirit whirled past me before fading away into the night. I fell backwards against the doorframe to get out of the way.

"Are you okay?" Jase pulled me upright.

I rubbed my elbow. I had knocked it on the edge of the door-jamb when she flashed past. "Yeah, I'm okay. But I can't believe she was in here all along!" I was confused.

Jase walked over and turned off the shower. "I know. But I swear she didn't come in through the door! Why is she following us if she doesn't want to interact with us?"

I wrapped my hair in my towel and squeezed the water out of it as we walked back outside. "Maybe she's trying to make us leave, the way the phantom pilot did at first."

He laughed harshly. "Why don't these phantoms just let us help them?"

I shrugged. "I'm more worried about all the racket she was making." I took the comb Jase offered, and began to drag it though my cold, wet hair.

"My folks probably think we were playing around or something . . ."

I nodded. "Okay," I said. "Hurry up."

Jase looked at me, misunderstanding creasing his face. "What for?"

"Your shower," I replied. "You better make it short though, cause if she comes back out here, I'm coming in there with you!"

Jase threw his head back and laughed. "Don't worry. I'm going to wait until tomorrow morning." He smiled softly. "No way I'm leaving you out there in the dark, alone. Especially not after she was so *volatile!*"

I exhaled audibly. "Thank you! Good word, by the way." I liked it when Jase came up with his big "writer" words. Besides, I didn't want to completely admit that I would have been terrified to stand out there alone.

When we returned, his folks were sitting in camp chairs near the fire. His Dad had the old guitar across his lap, but he wasn't playing anything. His mom was holding an embroidery hoop in her lap. It appeared that she had been embroidering a pattern of stars and stripes on a white background. It was hard to tell now that darkness had fallen. I wondered if she was making a flag or something.

"I was just about to send out a search party," Mr. Lee said.

Jase leaned down and gently plucked the guitar from his dad's lap. He sat in one of the other chairs, and laid the instrument flat across his knees. I sat down across the fire from him, and listened while he picked out a few mournful notes. He plucked at the strings and then pulled a funny, shiny metal collar up over his forefinger so that he could glide up and down the strings as he plucked. He must have had the thing in his pocket. Now it was sort of like a steel guitar.

I shivered. I couldn't tell if it was from the music, the coldness of my long hair on my skin, or from the encounter with the spirit woman.

Jase said, "I bought a song book at the music store." He started the chorus of an old Hank Williams' song called "I'm So Lonesome I Could Cry." But it was so sad that he only played a few notes before he switched to "She'll Be Coming 'Round the Mountain." When he went into "Old MacDonald Had a Farm," we all joined in. Soon we were laughing and quacking, oinking, and mooing, and it was so funny that I completely forgot about my spirits. Even Nasty Nora.

It wasn't until the fire began to die down, after we'd made and eaten our s'mores, that I finally let my mind wander back to the awful encounter. Of course, it wasn't the only time Jase and I had experienced a run-in with a ghost. First, it was the phantom pilot, Roger Gilpin, who had crashed his small plane behind Jase's house. He'd actually hung around—even peering out of Jase's closet from time to time. That's how Jase and I became friends, because he'd seem me going in the old haunted Taylor house, and that had made him think I was brave. I'm not brave, but I agreed to help him anyway, and thank goodness I did. He's been my best friend ever since.

Now that I think of it, the way all that worked out makes me think it was scripted by Fate or something. Then there was the incident of the phantom student in the old abandoned elementary school. Once again, it was as if the phantom appeared in response to an outside force—this time it was our new friend, Derol Pavey who needed help.

Now, miles and miles from home, we were seeing another phantom. I wondered if there was really something to the baby doll story. Seems awfully coincidental for a phantom to be searching for something at the very place folks have heard a baby crying, for *decades*.

I separated my hair into three even sections and braided it quickly. It was still damp so I knew it would be super-wavy the next day, but I couldn't worry about that right now. It was too cold lying across my shoulders.

As I worked, I thought about how Jase had once said he thought we'd opened a door to the other side when we helped Mr. Gilpin—the phantom pilot—reunite with his lost fiancée. But I think that spirit door was opened even earlier, when Jase had discovered Lady, the German shepherd, lying mangled beside the road. Turned out she also had a connection to Mr. Gilpin.

AFTER OUR S'MORES, we cleaned up and brushed our teeth with a bucket of water from the hydrant near the bathrooms. We didn't use lake water for this, not even boiled, although Mr. Lee kept telling me we were. He loved to tease me. I loved it, too. It reminded me of my Gramps.

I didn't think I would be able to sleep after everything that had happened, but once I'd crawled into my sleeping bag, I began to drift off almost immediately. Mrs. Lee's voice was so soothing as she knelt on her sleeping bag and murmured her prayers into her folded hands. Of course I couldn't make out everything she said, nor did I want to, but I could pick out Rusty's name, and Jase's, and once I thought I even heard mine. That made me feel . . . comfortable.

I slipped into sleep, exhausted.

I DON'T KNOW how long I slept before the baby doll came into the tent. I thought that was odd, because I'd seen Mrs. Lee tie the flap securely before turning

in. Nevertheless, I watched in horror as the thing crawled through the flap and then stood up and looked for me with its one good eye. The sightless eye was half-closed just the way it had been when I'd wrapped my shirt around it earlier.

Even as it was walking toward me, arms outstretched, I was telling myself this couldn't be happening—not that the thing couldn't be walking, that seemed logical enough—but that it couldn't be here because not only was the tent flap tied shut, *the doll was securely locked in the trunk of the car.*

That fact finally made me sit up.

It was still coming toward me. My old tee shirt was tangled around one of its baby feet, and the sound it made dragging that shirt across the floor—*swush, swush, swush*—seemed to be burrowing into my skull.

I slapped my hands over my ears and squeezed my eyes shut, but that was worse. I opened them quickly.

I couldn't *not* look.

It was getting closer. It was going to trip over Mrs. Lee.

My mind protested what I was seeing as the baby doll, never

taking its one good eye off me, fell down on its hands and knees and crawled onto Mrs. Lee's chest.

I knew I was about to scream.

I felt the sound building inside my own chest, working its way to my throat as the baby dragged itself, and my shirt right, directly across Mrs. Lee's sleeping face. Once it cleared the obstacle, it stood up and began the final trek toward me. There were only a couple of feet between our sleeping bags.

I opened my mouth—

"Wahhmahh."

That sound cut off any I would have made.

Mrs. Lee sat up. "Stevie? Was that you? What is it, dear?"

I looked at the doll still reaching out for me. Its mouth was open: "*Wahh—*"

I shoved myself out of my sleeping bag and vaulted over the one eyed doll. Its plastic fingers began to open and close on thin air as it tried to grasp the hem of my pajamas.

"Stevie-girl?" Mrs. Lee's voice sounded befuddled. I thought I saw her swipe a stray lock of hair off her forehead in an eerie imitation of her son.

But it was difficult to tell. The one sliver of moonlight that fell through the gaping tent flap lay directly upon the doll.

"What's wrong? Are you having a bad dream?" Her voice was beginning to sound impatient.

I looked around for the baby doll, but it had somehow vanished.

"I don't . . . I'm not sure . . ." I glanced down at my sleeping bag. *Could it be in there?* I didn't see any bulge. But it had seemed so *real*.

I glanced at the tent flap. It was definitely pulled aside as if something had entered.

"Come here, Stevie," Mrs. Lee patted her own sleeping bag. "Would you like to talk about it?"

Embarrassed, I sat beside her. I most certainly did *not* want to talk about it, but I didn't want to be rude. "Would it be all right if I don't talk about it?" My breath was still caught up in my throat. Behind me, the bottom of the tent was also pulled up a bit. A stream of cool night air wended its way between us.

I shivered.

Mrs. Lee took her own flannel robe and wrapped it snugly around my shoulders. "There, that will help." She gave me a little hug and then reached across and tugged my sleeping bag closer to hers.

I eyed it warily. There were no bulges in the fabric.

In a way, I thought I should protest. Here I was, going on fourteen, about to start high school, and my best friend's mom was comforting me as if I were a kindergartner. On the other hand, I *was* the one who spread the blanket across her and Jase when the Military Chaplain had brought the awful news about Rusty. I guess we'd both seen each other at our lowest.

"Thanks," I whispered. I crawled back into my sleeping bag still wrapped in her robe.

After a few quiet moments, she said, "It was that doll, wasn't it?"

I almost died. Had it been real? If not, then how did she know?

"Yes, ma'am," I replied. "I – I guess it was just a bad dream."

She didn't argue, or try to tell me everything would be okay.

In fact, we didn't talk anymore, at all.

I was still awake when the first strip of daylight teased the gaping tent flap, so I gave up and slipped out of my sleeping bag, and the flannel robe.

Mrs. Lee was snoring softly.

5

I couldn't wait to tell Jase about the dream. I thought briefly about asking him to look in the trunk and make sure the thing was still there, but I couldn't think of a way to do that without telling Mr. Lee why I wanted the key.

When I peeked out of my tent flap, Jase was already stacking new twigs and branches into a pyramid inside our fire-ring.

"Morning." His deep voice was rough.

It was so strange, waking up in the woods and seeing Jase before I'd even had a chance to go to the bathroom or look into a mirror. Not that I wasn't used to him being at my house early in the morning because I was. We always rode our bikes to school together and he would often come in and have breakfast with us, but this was different. It was out of our routine.

"Headed to the bathrooms," I said. I'd been very worried about going back down to the bathroom after last night's episode, but with Jase beside me, it would be okay. I hoped. I decided I wouldn't tell him about the baby doll dream until we were on our way back. It was still too fresh in my mind, and I knew it was going to be difficult enough to go inside the bathroom without adding any more scary images to the mix inside my head.

He laid the last dry branch on his pyramid and fell into step beside me, but for once, he wasn't smiling.

"What's wrong?" I asked.

Jase swiped his blond hair off his forehead automatically. "Dreamed about that bridge."

I waited a moment to see if he'd say more. But the only thing making noise was a mockingbird trilling and chirping from a branch somewhere up the trail. "Was it about the woman?" I asked at last.

Jase shook his head. He couldn't seem to bring himself to tell me the rest.

"What was it then?" I stuck my hands in my back pockets and tried to sound nonchalant, but inside, I grew cold.

"It was Rusty." His voice was no longer deep and rough, now it sounded like someone else's voice altogether. "He was standing on a bridge sort of like Crybaby Bridge. It was all misty underneath, and he – he was misty, too."

I inhaled sharply. "Oh, Jase . . ."

"I think he was a ghost."

My cold insides took over my outsides and I rubbed my hands up and down my arms in an attempt to rub away the chills. "Did he say anything?"

Jase shook his head and swiped at his nose. "He just kept looking off into the forest, as if he was listening for something. Only it kind of looked like the jungle instead of the forest. It was dark. Hard to tell."

I looped my arm into the crook of his elbow and hugged it to my side.

"Do you think that means he's dead?" His voice caught on the word dead, reminding me of the way the baby doll had caught up in the tangle of branches at the edge of the creek. "Do you think that was really him?"

I laid my cheek against his shoulder and hugged his arm even tighter. It wouldn't be wise to answer abruptly. "Maybe it was just a bad dream." I looked up at his face. "We don't *always* see phantoms."

We walked on without speaking, the chatter of the mocking-bird echoing behind us like an exclamation point at the end of a sentence.

The bathroom was deserted. The only evidence of our experience from the night before was the damaged place in the tile. I glanced around as I hurried toward the stalls, but I didn't see the little chip anywhere. Maybe someone had swept up last night or this morning. It certainly looked and smelled clean.

Jase stayed outside the door just like before. For a second, I thought about backing out and waiting until Mrs. Lee woke up. I was pretty sure nothing would happen if she were here, but after last night, I really didn't want to admit to her that not only was I afraid to go to sleep alone, now I was afraid to go to the bathroom alone.

I let the door close behind me.

I decided I'd rather take my chances with the phantom.

I slid inside the first stall soundlessly.

There was no puddle of lake water on the floor and the lid to the toilet was up so I knew the cleaning crew had been here. I carefully lowered the lid and unsnapped my jeans. The toilet seat was so cold, and I was so nervous, I thought I would never go—should have turned on the faucet, I thought. But finally, I did my business, went out, washed my hands, and glanced into the mirror to check my hair and face.

For a moment, I thought of the little phantom of the schoolhouse. She had first contacted me by appearing in my bathroom mirror at home—but no. This time there was no phantom. It was just me gazing back.

I exhaled a sigh of relief, pulled my toothbrush from my back pocket and quickly brushed my teeth. After I did a quick swish and rinse, I shook the water from the toothbrush and whirled around, excited to rush out and tell Jase everything was okay.

Nora was standing directly behind me.

I gasped and stepped back instinctively. My bottom hit the edge of the sink. "Nora, thank goodness." I was relieved it was only her and not the woman in white. "You scared me!"

In the back of my mind, I was already scolding Jase for letting her through so silently. I thought he would at least make some sort of loud noise to let me know someone was coming in. Especially after last night.

"You shouldn't have taken the baby," she said. Then she flung open the bathroom door and walked out leaving me speechless.

Close your mouth, Stevie-girl, Gramps would've said; you'll catch a fly.

Instead, I caught the door before it closed completely. Jase was staring at her as she walked off down the trail toward the store.

"How come you didn't warn me?" I asked, my hand on my hip.

"Warn you?" He obviously didn't know what I meant.

I laughed. "I thought that's why you were guarding the door. To tell me if someone was coming in."

"She didn't."

My head jerked up. "Didn't?"

Jase shook his head. "She didn't come past me. I was right here the whole time."

A bird trilled and was silent. The leaves rustled in the treetops.

"She must have already been in there." He wasn't accusing, just stating an obvious fact.

"You're right." I thought about how I'd crept in so quietly, but hadn't even bothered to check all the stalls this time. "She must've been in one of the other stalls." I shook myself. "It was just creepy. She said I shouldn't have taken the doll."

"That's it? That's all she said?" Jase was gazing toward the trail as if he wanted to follow her.

"Yeah . . ." I thought for a second. "Only she didn't say doll—she said baby. She said I shouldn't have taken the *baby*."

"Curioser and curioser," Jase said, quoting Lewis Carroll, author of *Alice in Wonderland.*

"Did this sort of thing happen any of the other times y'all camped here?" I felt like it was a stupid question, the answer obviously being no, or he would have mentioned it.

He just shook his head. "Never, well, almost never." His eye strayed toward the trail again. The bridge was down that trail.

"Almost?" I tucked the tip of my messy braid into the corner of my mouth, a habit I'd been trying to break for some time.

"It was nothing. Not really." The tone of his voice belied his words.

I'd come to recognize the flat tone his voice often took on whenever he wasn't being completely forthright—like the night he decided to go back inside the old schoolhouse even though we were pretty certain someone was hiding inside the locked pantry.

"What was it?" I asked.

He was about to duck into the men's side of the bathrooms. "Just thought I heard the baby cry one time, that's all." He pushed the door open. "Didn't say anything when it happened . . . didn't want Rusty to think I was a *crybaby*." He looked at me seriously. "And I didn't want to scare you by telling you. I was afraid you wouldn't come with us." His face was turned away. "That's why I told you I hadn't heard it before." He quickly slipped through the gap and let the door close behind him.

That's all? That's all! Sheesh. I wonder what else he hasn't told me?

I KEPT watch outside the bathroom, contemplating the woods and all the things Jase had said. Thinking about everything that had happened so far.

Nothing would surprise me now. In fact, I told myself I was prepared for whatever might happen next.

But nothing else did.

Before Jase came out, I heard his Dad coming down the lane from the direction of camp.

"Mornin', Stevie-girl! How'd you sleep?"

Mrs. Lee was beside him. She smiled warmly, as if to tell me our secret was safe.

I smiled back at them. "I slept pretty well," I fibbed.

Jase appeared, shaking out his toothbrush. "What're we doing for breakfast, Dad?" His voice boomed in the early morning quiet.

"Flapjacks," his dad replied. "My specialty."

Jase rubbed his hands together. "Great! Stevie and I will get the fire started—"

I knew he already had the campfire built; all we'd have to do is light the tinder. "Race you!" I called, taking off without waiting to see if he was coming. I needed a huge head start, and I took it.

We arrived back at camp out of breath, with me still in the lead.

"You cheated!" He was laughing.

"Not cheating." I laughed. "Just evening the odds. I think in sports it's called handicapping."

"You read too much, Stevie-girl. Handicapping and cheating, not the same thing—"

"I did not cheat!" I tried to make my voice sound indignant. "You wouldn't let an Arabian thoroughbred race a Shetland pony would you?"

Jase laughed so hard he doubled over, tears squeezing from the corners of his eyes. "Me being the thoroughbred and you being the Shetlan—"

"Okay, okay," I said. "That was a bad example . . ." I tried to change the subject. But I'd put my foot in my mouth, and he wasn't about to let me take it out.

"Whee-hee-hee-he," he whinnied, making me laugh and cringe all at the same time. "Whee-hee—" His mocking whinny cut off abruptly.

I stopped piling the dried moss beneath the pyramid of sticks and followed his gaze.

He was staring at the trunk of the car.

The lid was slightly raised.

A sudden chill gripped me so violently my teeth clamped together with a snap.

We looked at each other across the unlit campfire, and then we both started toward the car as if one of us had called the other.

"Wait," I said, my dream surfacing like a shark in a calm sea.

Jase stopped in his tracks, a question on his face.

"I never told you about my dream last night . . ." I swallowed. "It even woke your mom."

He stood patiently.

My eyes fastened on the slice of darkness visible beneath the barely opened lid of the trunk. "The baby doll walked into our tent last night, it was dragging my shirt behind it."

Jase's expression would have been comical if he hadn't been standing only two feet from the partially open trunk.

"What's going on?" Mr. Lee's voice jolted us back to reality.

We looked at him and then at the car.

A frown creased his brow. "How'd that get open?" He ran his hand into his pants pocket and pulled out the key.

Jase walked over, flipped up the lid, and peered into the storage area. "Nothing in here but the spare," he said. I thought I detected the slightest hint of a tremor in his voice.

I crossed the camp and looked in. Even my shirt was gone. There was a slightly darker area of carpet where the doll had been. I pressed my palm down onto the spot. It was still damp.

"Guess I didn't close it all the way," Mr. Lee said. Then he smashed it down.

We all heard the hearty clunk when the lock engaged.

"Nora must have come looking for it."

I glanced at Mrs. Lee. Her face was pale, but she smiled wanly. "I guess she saw the open trunk and found the doll."

I shrugged as if it were no big deal.

Jase plowed one hand into his shaggy hair. "That's gotta be it."

6

*A*fter a long, leisurely breakfast—during which no one mentioned the doll—we all voted to drive around the lake to the place where they rented paddleboats. I could see the glint in Jase and Mr. Lee's eyes. They were gearing up for a competition; I just knew it.

I couldn't believe our time here was going by so fast. Only a couple more days, and then it would be back to the real world for us. In a way, I was looking forward to that because I got a vague uneasy feeling every time I thought of my Gramps. I told myself it was just worry at being away from him for so long. But whatever it was, the feeling would not go away. I tried to convince myself it was just because of all the weird stuff that kept happening.

Eventually, I believed it.

On the other hand, I was having such a good time with the Lee family I did not look forward to going back to our routine lives. Especially not without solving the mystery of the woman in white.

This time, on the paddleboat outing, Mrs. Lee did not pack a picnic for our lunch. Mr. Lee told us to take a second set of clothes so that we could go into the lakeside restaurant to eat dinner before we returned.

"Is this another tradition?" I asked.

Jase nodded.

Once again, we were in the back seat while his dad drove us to the rent-a-boat site. We rented two paddleboats and spent three hours exploring the lake. Of course Jase and his dad had to race each other a time or two—but they finally stopped after each had won. Thank goodness. Even though it was almost exactly the same as peddling a bike, I didn't think my legs could "peddle" that paddleboat much more. It was impossible to go as fast as Jase wanted.

It *was* gorgeous though. The lake was huge and pristine. And in a couple of places, the trees hugged the shore so densely that it would have been impossible for us to pull up and set foot on land.

Once or twice, I got that wrinkly feeling on the back of my neck.

I wanted to turn around and see if someone, or something, was watching from the bank, but Jase was a stern taskmaster. If I lagged, he pushed the pedals on his side of the boat even harder to make up for it. Before I knew it, all my drinking water was gone and I was sneaking drinks from his canteen.

I was glad when Mrs. Lee motioned for us to turn around and head back to the rental place.

The man who was in charge remembered the Lee's from their earlier trips, but he didn't know about Rusty.

"What about your other boy?" he called out as we tied our boats to the pier. "He grown and gone now?"

I saw Mr. Lee's back stiffen as he rose from securing the boat. Mrs. Lee laid her palm on his shoulder. I wasn't sure if she was touching him in support, or to keep him from turning around and giving the man a piece of his mind just for mentioning Rusty's name.

Fortunately, Jae and I were standing nearer to the man. "Rusty went to Vietnam," Jase said quietly. "His 'copter was shot down a few months ago." His green eyes drifted to the sky as he spoke. "He's listed as Missing in Action."

I could almost feel the man's remorse seeping out of his pores. I could tell by the way he reacted that he never would have said what he did if he'd had any idea. "Sorry to hear that," he mumbled. "Prayers are with you . . ."

I think we were all glad when a young couple with a small boy arrived and asked about renting one of the boats we'd just returned.

The mosquitoes were beginning to flock to us as if to a smorgasbord. I slapped at them uncomfortably.

Mr. and Mrs. Lee were walking ahead of us. It felt as if the fun had seeped out of the day. I thought I saw Mr. Lee wiping something off his face a time or two, but it was probably just perspiration or lake water.

Jase broke the silence at last. "You'll like the restaurant. It's right on the edge of the river where it pours over the dam and into the lake."

He grasped my hand lightly. I gave his fingers a little squeeze and he smiled crookedly, but the smile never really reached his eyes. I squeezed even harder and we walked on in silence.

Our suits were already dry by the time we reached the car—we had only gotten off the paddleboats once, way out in the deep part of the lake—and I hadn't lasted very long. The water there was very dark and very cold. I didn't like not knowing where the bottom was. Jase said he thought it was forty to fifty feet deep. Something about that really bothered me, and when an unseen fish brushed my leg, I scrambled back onto the boat and didn't go in again. I didn't even want my feet dangling in the water after that.

We'd seen a fence near the camp store where fishermen hung catfish heads all in a row. Some of those heads boasted mouths wide enough to swallow basketballs. Plus, I'd overheard the store owner telling Mr. Lee that one of the dam inspectors claimed to have seen a catfish the size of a Holstein calf the last time he had dived down to the bottom of the dam to inspect it.

As we swam, I remember picturing a huge catfish beneath our little paddleboat. In my mind, it was large enough to swallow us all.

It was only after I had clambered back onto the boat that I noticed Mrs. Lee hadn't gone for a swim either. She was sitting patiently, reading a paperback book she must have had in her tote bag, while Jase and Mr. Lee tried to see who could dive the deepest. Apparently both of us girls shared a fear of the unknown.

Mr. Lee stopped at the public restrooms and we all went inside and pulled our clean clothes on over our dry suits. The kid in me really liked this lake living, but every once in a while, I wondered if I should worry about how red my face was getting, or how messy my braid looked. I glanced at the mirror, but it was one of those sheets of polished metal and I couldn't tell much.

Jase was right. I *loved* the restaurant. The patio area was built right out over the dam, and it was screened on all sides so no pesky flies or mosquitoes could bother us. But the best part was the sound of the water rushing over the barrier. It was like a waterfall. It was so loud we could barely hear each other.

Of course we were all famished.

By the time we'd eaten our fill—I had a patty melt with French fries and Jase had a club sandwich that was so big he almost couldn't fit it in his mouth, plus half my fries—I was one tired girl.

I think it was a good thing the rushing water was so loud. Mr. and Mrs. Lee didn't seem to want conversation, and Jase and I were too busy stuffing our faces to talk.

On the way back to camp, we drove directly into the setting sun. It was like a picture show. The sky was streaked with clouds that appeared to be burning from underneath. The gorgeous combination of pink and gold made me think of Heaven.

I must have dozed. I only came awake when Jase touched my hand and told me we were back at camp. I crawled into my sleeping bag and changed into my pajamas in the darkness. Mrs. Lee came in with a flashlight a few moments later, but I was so groggy I barely opened my eyes. All I remember is how she patted my shoulder and told me she was glad I had come on the trip. Then I conked out. All that peddling, trying to keep up with Jase, had worn me out.

Threads of lightning stitched through the night, sewing together fragments of the sky the booming thunder had blown apart. Rain streamed over me in frigid sheets. I wiped my eyes again and again, trying to clear my vision long enough to see what the woman was doing on the bridge.

She was on the opposite end, shrouded in rain and shadows. She appeared to be yelling into the storm, her hands cupped around her mouth. Her dress was plastered to her body like a thin white skin.

I wiped at my eyes and started forward, looking back to make certain Jase was with me. But I couldn't see him. Maybe he was ahead of me again. *When had the storm begun?* I walked and walked and walked, but I couldn't make it to the center of the bridge. The rain was so fierce . . . the bridge seemed to have lengthened.

"Jase?" I called and listened. I couldn't hear anything. Was he back there or not?

I turned around once more, pushing my heavy hair off my face. *That* wasn't right, my hair was in a braid. It wasn't over my face, and *where was Jase?* Why couldn't I see him?

A cracking sound penetrated my confused thoughts as another loud boom of thunder crashed through the air flattening my eardrums as surely as if I'd dropped to the bottom of the loop on a roller coaster.

"Jase!" I screamed. The lightning lit up the night and I saw what had made the awful cracking sound. The bridge was going. The creek had swelled beyond its banks. Huge trees and the roof of someone's house had smacked into the wooden stanchions. A loud grinding noise reached my ears as the thick timbers began to give way under the onslaught. It felt as if things were happening in slow motion.

Where was the woman? I couldn't see her anymore. The rain was coming down so hard it hurt my eyes and I shut them against the onslaught. The rain stung my cheeks. I forced my eyelids open again, but something wasn't right; there was no rain, no storm, no weather. I was in my sleeping bag, inside the tent with Jase's mom.

I rolled over, searching for some tiny glimmer of light in the darkness. I was certain I'd opened my eyes, but everything was still solid black. I raised my hand to touch that blackness, positive it must be some sort of fabric, a curtain someone had strung across the middle of the tent perhaps. My hand just went on and on into the darkness. And it was *cold*.

I gasped at the frigid mist enveloping my hand. It felt as if I were reaching inside an open freezer. I wanted to call out, but what would Mrs. Lee think if I did? She'd think I was nuts. *Maybe I am . . .*

Pulling my hand back into the warmth of my sleeping bag, I gingerly reached up and felt of my face. My eyes were open.

I must be *blind*. I'd read about hysterical blindness. That had to be it. The nightmare about the storm had somehow struck me blind. No darkness could be this complete. Where was the moon? The stars? There were several gaps around the tent flap, and even at the bottom of the tent. What was going on?

I'm not awake. That has to be it. I'm still dreaming. I let out a gentle sigh of relief. Dreaming, that's all—

Something crawled across my face . . . something small, like a roly-poly bug.

I slapped at my cheek and shook my head violently. I couldn't help it; I cried out.

"What is it, dear?"

Was that Jase's mom?

Her voice didn't sound right. It sounded thick and phlegmy, full of watery mold.

I sat up just as *she* loomed out of nowhere, her white fish-eaten face crawling with raindrops like tiny clear bugs under the skin.

It wasn't Jase's mom at all.

It was the woman in white and she was in my tent, in my space, in my face, she was leaning down—

I woke up.

Finally.

And opened my eyes.

And she was still there, her drowned, sightless eyes staring whitely into mine, her fetid breath soggy upon my cheek because she was so close I think she was trying to steal my breath and suck it down into her poor useless water-clogged lungs . . .

I screamed and choked and sat up struggling for breath and

for air and for sanity because how many times must one awake before becoming conscious?

Then at last I could see the tiny slivers of moonlight that signified the gaps around our tent flap. For a second, I debated lying back down, trying to go back to sleep, but I knew that wasn't going to happen. Every time I closed my eyes, I wondered if she would be there when I opened them again.

Had she really been there?

I'd had dealings with phantoms, even a shadow-man who probably would have hurt one of us if Billy Bob and Mr. Pearcy hadn't arrived when they did, but I'd never encountered anything like these nightmares. If it wasn't the baby doll, it was the woman in white. But she wasn't like a see-through phantom. She was more like a walking, dripping, corpse.

That convinced me. I had to get some fresh air. I didn't want to go traipsing around the campsite in the middle of the night, I knew that wasn't a good idea, but I thought if I could just open the tent flap, let a little air inside, maybe take a drink of cool water from my canteen, look at the stars . . . I always got up and went to the window at home when I couldn't sleep. Something about the moonlight comforted me.

Too bad I hadn't brought Gran's old afghan to curl up in. That would have made me feel better.

Carefully, I untied the lacing holding the canvas door flap closed. A nice little breeze immediately crept inside. I inhaled deeply. Through the split I could see a cozy three-quarter moon. It shone through the darkness like a glorious nightlight.

A movement caught my attention. A tall figure rose from the darkness on the opposite side of the cold campfire. The shaggy blond hair and rangy frame told me it was Jase.

"You okay?" Jase's voice was soft.

I nodded. Just seeing him made me feel better.

Quiet as fog, I slipped out of the tent and joined him in the moonlight.

"Another bad dream." I rinsed my mouth with water from my canteen, and then took another sip. "You couldn't sleep either?"

He shook his head, sat back down, and opened one side of his scratchy Army blanket so that I could sit beside him. He wrapped the blanket around the two of us like a shawl. I snuggled under his armpit, a little chick snuggling beneath warm feathers.

"Have you slept at all?"

He shrugged. "Mostly I just lay there listening to dad snore. Thought I heard you call out once. What was the dream?"

I shook my head vehemently. "I'll tell you when it's light, not in the darkness." I shivered. "Someone *really* doesn't want me here."

He pulled me closer. "That bad, huh?"

I nodded without speaking.

The nightscape was brilliant, the moon luminous. When I gazed out across the campsite with its fallen logs edging the fire, and the beach area leading down to the water, it appeared very foreign, as if we were *on* the moon—or some other planet, perhaps.

The lake was smooth, not glassy, too shadowy for that, but it seemed to be molten, some kind of liquid metal swaying gently in its wide, wide bed. Every now and then I could hear a burble as the gentle current laughed to itself as it tickled the shoreline, but it wasn't a bad sound. It was actually quite soothing. The aroma of lake water and pine was a balm for my battered senses. I felt myself growing sleepy in my warm little nest.

The dream had been horrific, but I suspected there was a kernel of truth buried inside it. I would have to examine it tomorrow. Right now, I was just too content.

We slept sitting up with our backs against the biggest log. Sunrise surprised us with birdsong, and when I felt Jase moving beside me, stretching his long arms and legs, I looked up into his handsome face.

I knew what was about to happen.

I closed my eyes and felt the barest brush of his lips on mine.

My first real kiss.

Perfect.

I snuggled into his side once more and he hugged me tightly.

No words were necessary.

Mr. Lee yawned loudly as he clambered, stretching, from his tent. "Morning kids." His voice was cheery, but not loud. "You two are up early. Ready to go catch our breakfast?"

We grinned at each other. "You bet," we said in unison.

I didn't care a whit about catching fish, but I really enjoyed watching this new camaraderie developing between Jase and his dad. Or maybe I should say redeveloping, because I'm sure it had been there all along. It just took the tragedy of Rusty going missing to bring it to the forefront again.

If anyone had asked me, which of course they didn't, I would have said that Rusty's crash and disappearance would have driven an even broader wedge between Mr. and Mrs. Lee and Jase, but it seemed to have done just the opposite. It was as if the worst had now happened and they were being forced to move on or give up entirely.

I was very glad they'd chosen to move on.

7

*W*e caught two fish almost as soon as our hooks hit the water. Mr. Lee laughed and pulled mine off the hook while I stood behind Jase with my eyes covered. Wading into the shallow water in the early morning stillness, I discovered I was wrong, again. I *did* care a whit about catching fish.

The woods had awakened around us as we stood in the cool early air, ankle deep in the gentle current. Thankfully, the insects seemed to have slept in. I stood there between Jase and his dad, and I knew there wouldn't be another morning like this. When I glanced at Jase, one hand shading my eyes against the brightness, he grinned and my heart stuttered in my chest just like the water stuttered over the rocks in the creek.

Even the fish for breakfast tasted much better than I thought possible. In fact, I had been downright leery about it as a breakfast food—until the smell of it sizzling in the skillet hit my nose—then my stomach had awoken and there was no turning back.

Mrs. Lee made cottage fries to go along with it, and by the time it was ready, I made a complete pig of myself. And it didn't bother me at all.

It didn't take us long to clean up since there wasn't much left, and now we were headed back to the lake trail for some hiking.

In the bright morning light, my nightmare had faded away like the camp smoke on the breeze.

We were just entering the well-worn trail when I spied a familiar form coming toward us.

I couldn't believe it.

Karla?

Could it really be my old best friend, Karla, coming down the trail? It looked like her, but her blond hair was almost white, and those shorts, holy *carumba*. They were *short*. And that eye shadow, so shockingly *blue* and sparkly.

But it was, it *was* Karla. My best friend in the whole wide world was here.

Somehow, she was here, in the woods.

I flew down the path and smashed into her, embracing her in a bear hug to end all bear hugs. *Wow*, she had really filled out.

"Karla!" I cried. "What are you doing here? I'm so glad to see you!"

"Stevie!" She embraced me back, and then held me at arm's length. "You got *tall*."

I guess we'd both grown. Only she had filled out like a girl was supposed to. I'd just gotten taller.

"And who is this hunk?" Her eyes fastened on Jase.

I saw his cheeks flush with embarrassment.

"Jason Lee," he said, holding out his hand formally. "Pleased to meet you. Stevie told me about you."

Karla grasped his hand and rolled her marble-blue eyes. Her eye shadow glittered like diamond dust in the sun. "I hope she didn't tell you everything. At least not *all* the bad stuff!" She giggled when she said that, and I recalled how her last couple of letters, which had been very far apart, had been all about drinking and partying on the beach and how "far" she'd gone with her boyfriend, Charlie.

Charlie and Karlie, I thought, how funny.

"What are you *doing* here?" I noticed she was still holding onto Jase's hand. "Did Charlie bring you?" In her last letter, she'd bragged about how Charlie had his own car.

"No-*o-o.*" She laughed, making the word tinkle like a bell. "I don't go with Charlie anymore. He got his license revoked." She dropped Jase's hand and took hold of his upper arm instead. Then she completely turned her back to me and smiled up at Jase. "I don't even *have* a boyfriend anymore." When she looked my way again, her bottom lip was stuck out in a ridiculous pout.

I was dumbfounded. What was she *doing*? Was she flirting with Jase? She knew who he was. I'd told her all about him in my letters. I thought she understood.

My face filled with hot blood. I started toward them, but just then her mom came clomping toward us carrying a picnic basket and a tote bag.

"There you are," her mom said. "Stevie, come here! I am so glad to see you." She hugged the stuffing out of me. "We've missed you so *much*." Her voice was loud in the middle of the forest trail. "When Karla told me you were camping here, I made it a point to reserve a camp spot for us for tonight. We're on our way to Crossroads to visit my brother. Karla's dad is coming home, we may even be moving back. Isn't that wonderful?"

Had her voice always been so brassy? So *shrill*? Or had she seen how Karla was acting? *Was she trying to make up for it by talking so fast and so loud?*

"That's wonderful." I said. "I've missed y'all, too." I returned her hug as best I could, but I couldn't make my voice sound jolly with Karla hanging onto Jase as if she was drowning and he was a rope.

I glanced at them again. Karla was still standing there, clutching his arm, her gaze glued to his face. She wasn't even trying to disguise her interest. As I watched, she squeezed his arm and said something too low for me to hear, something that ended in a flirty giggle.

I turned and started toward the campsite.

"Stevie? Stevie-girl?"

That was Karla's mom again.

"Be right back," I called over my shoulder. Tears of hurt and anger had popped into my eyes. I didn't want to be rude, but I'd be darned if I was going to let them see me cry. My best friend in the whole entire world had just come back into my life. I hadn't seen her in over two years, and yet, all she can do is make cow eyes at my . . . new best friend.

Before I knew it, I was running. In the back of my mind I wondered if I was giving in too easily. Shouldn't I stay and stick up for myself? She had no right to stroll in like some beach-blanket-bimbo and try to steal Jase away from me. Oh, I knew he wasn't really mine. We'd barely shared our first kiss. But it just wasn't fair. Karla was supposed to be my best friend in the *whole world*.

With friends like that, who needs enemies?

I stopped running, but I kept walking, and thinking. I knew I was acting like a child. But that feeling of utter betrayal was like a slow burning campfire inside my gut. *A real friend wouldn't act that way. A real friend would never flirt like that, especially one who had been gone for so long—*

More tears came suddenly and fiercely. They were so blinding I had to sit down to keep from running into tree branches.

I stepped off the trail and sat on a fallen log with my wet face buried in my hands. Sobbing, I let myself slip all the way down to the ground, hidden behind the log. The tears felt hot, shameful. *No one has died. No one is going to die. Stop being such a baby. So she wasn't the friend you thought she was, maybe she just changed. It doesn't mean she was never your friend. After all, you have lots more friends now that she's gone. And look how much you've changed!*

Good old common sense, talking at me again . . . so many things going on in my head, and in my heart, and deep down in my gut where the real me lived.

I lifted the edge of my tank top and dried my face. When I opened my eyes, right in front of me, poison ivy. Ugh. I rose carefully, making absolutely certain I didn't brush it with my bare arms or legs.

I started back down the trail, careful to stay on the path this time. In my head, I kept going over differing scenarios of how to act around her now. I wished with all my heart that I'd never told her about this camping trip at all. Who would've thought her mom would actually come looking for me? Guess she thought we would really enjoy seeing each other. Especially since I wasn't going to be home when they visited her uncle in Crossroads.

And what if he likes her more than you? That's what you're really worried about, isn't it? Shut up, I told myself. Just shut up!

Feeling ridiculous for the way I had reacted, or perhaps over-reacted, I began to jog. Now that I'd had my little pity party, I was ready to go back and face her. She wasn't so great. She was just Karla, after all. So what if she had filled out in all the places I hadn't? I still knew her secrets, like how she thought her nose was too big, and how if she got a pimple she would freak out and squeeze it until it made an awful sore. Nope. She wasn't perfect, even if she did have bleach-bottle hair and a California tan.

After a few minutes, I realized I had no idea where I was.

I stopped, hands on my hips, and listened for the sound of running water. Where was the sound of Stutter Creek? Surely I hadn't got so turned around that I had lost the entire creek.

I dug an arrow in the earth with the heel of my shoe to show myself which way I'd been headed, and then I turned about in a slow circle. Nothing looked familiar. I couldn't even spot the fallen log with the poison ivy anymore, although I knew it had to be somewhere behind me.

Inhaling deeply, to fight the rising quell of panic, I glanced up toward the sky. The trees were so tall I couldn't find the sun. I couldn't even tell what part of the sky it was in. The daylight was diffuse, diluted, filtered by layer upon layer of leafy branches.

Slowly, I began to backtrack. I had only been jogging for a few minutes. I couldn't have gone very far. I forced myself into a sedate walk, taking note of everything I passed.

When I still hadn't reached the fallen log after walking and looking for what felt like at least half an hour, I began to worry. In scouts, when I was a kid, they'd taught us that if we were ever lost, we should stay in one place and wait for rescue. But I wasn't a kid any longer. Besides, I'd already been up and down the trail, so I'd blown that idea. *What now?*

I stood as still as possible and listened. I wanted to yell out, but I didn't want Her Royal Highness to know that I might be lost. I felt more like an idiot with each passing second. I couldn't believe I'd run off that way. Getting myself lost in the woods and then advertising it, too? Huh-uh. I'd walk around all night to avoid that scenario.

Slowly, I began to move forward again, keeping my eyes peeled for anything familiar. Surely Jase will wonder where I am when he goes back to camp and I'm not there. Won't he? Or will he be too captivated by HRH to notice? I walked on, heart heavy and footsore. I tried to find the sun again, but it was really hard to see.

Should I climb a tree?

I looked all around. The woods had completely lost their appeal.

I swatted at the gnats and mosquitoes attracted to the sweat on the back of my neck. They reminded me of the flies that had surrounded the garage at the old haunted Taylor mansion back home.

Everything was quiet except for the occasional rustle of a small animal like a squirrel, or the cheerful twitter of a bird. I placed my feet carefully, intent on preserving the solitude. This area was so devoid of humanity it felt almost holy, like a church with no one inside. Even the light streaming through the lacy canopy of trees seemed heavenly. I began to feel peaceful again, safe, as if someone were watching over me.

My breathing returned to normal. I rolled my head, flexed my shoulders, took another calming breath, and stepped on a dry branch.

The loud *c-r-a-c-k* almost gave me heart failure.

My flight instinct kicked in and it was all I could do not to take off running again. *Darn it! I had let my green-eyed monster get the best of me. Now look what a mess I'm—*

What was that?

I stopped as suddenly as if I'd stepped in quicksand. It wasn't a dry branch this time. It was a large sound, something forcing its way through the brush toward me.

A dark, slump-shouldered shape materialized in my peripheral vision.

Mr. Lee said there were no bears in these woods.

I wanted to turn my head and examine the shape, but I was certain if I looked too closely, it would come for me. If I didn't look at it, maybe it wouldn't see me. Maybe it would just keep going.

Be still, just be still . . .

Did it move?

Did it?

My neck was so stiff with fear the muscles practically creaked when I forced myself to look.

It was still the same. It hadn't moved.

The blackness under the bushes was the perfect shadow-cave. I couldn't really see anything—

Then, suddenly, I could.

I could see sharp, white teeth in a black snout. A feral smile . . .

I began to run. Not only did my feet unfreeze, they took on a life of their own. It was all I could do to keep from crashing headlong into low-hanging branches and forearm-grabbing brambles.

Was it coming?

I looked over my shoulder just as the biggest tree root in the history of mankind seized the toe of my sneaker and threw me to the ground. The breath was knocked out of my chest with a *whump* that felt even worse than it sounded.

Coughing, trying to suck in enough air to get to my feet, I somehow managed to flip onto my back rather than continue to lie on my belly and wait to be devoured.

My chest felt compressed, as if the bear had caught up and was sitting on me.

I whipped my head around, searching for the huge shape, but here was nothing. Nothing was slavering over me with sharp white teeth. Nothing was charging after me out of the gloom, kicking up little puffets of dust from the rich brown earth of the trail. There wasn't even anything moving in the underbrush.

I forced myself to a sitting position and drew in another ragged breath. When I fell, I had landed flat on my chest with barely an instant to put my hands down to break the fall. That's what they mean by getting the breath knocked out of you, I thought. Then I let my head dip down between my knees as everything went gray.

I willed myself not to pass out.

In a few seconds, the world came back into color—like Dorothy arriving in the Land of Oz—and with it came the fear.

What was that thing? Was it a "mad" dog? *Nah, that's just a story my Gran used to tell.* I remembered the story clearly, how she'd been walking home from a friend's house *(at least she'd had a friend)* after dark one night, barefoot because they didn't buy shoes during the summer months, and something had started to follow her. She was convinced that the something was a mad dog, a dog with rabies like their little farm-dog, Tipper, who had contracted the horrific disease the previous year.

I stopped that train of thought and slowly looked around. Nothing was following me; nothing was sitting in the underbrush, red eyes glowing like little coals. No white teeth were shining out of a feral snout...

I began to feel better. *It was just my imagination, as the Temptations' said.* I began to whisper-sing the lyrics. Singing usually made me feel better. Took my mind off my problems.

I stood carefully. It required some effort. I was truly surprised at how difficult it was to recover just from getting the wind knocked out of me. I remembered all the times I'd seen football players helped from the field during our Friday night games. The announcer would say, "He'll be all right, folks. Just got the wind knocked out of him." Now I know how that feels, and I think the announcers should be scolded for their jovial tones.

I stood a little straighter, drew in a bit more air, and then I put one foot in front of the other, determined not to panic. My chest still felt compressed, caved in. But my main concern was figuring out what had scared me in the first place. I knew I'd seen something. My imagination might have made it move, might have made me think it was chasing me, but I was certain there was something there to begin with.

What happens if it gets dark? Then what?

I won't think of that, I told myself. One step at a time. One foot in front of the other. My head was pounding from my fall; not bad, not a sharp stabbing pain, just a constant little drum beat to let me know how stupid I had been. Just enough to let me know that a drink of water would be very helpful. My crazed dashings had left me dry and depleted.

Won't think of that, either.

I began to hum "Me and Bobby McGee," the Janis Joplin tune Jase had been strumming beside the campfire. Of course, that made me think of him and how sweet our first kiss had been—*was that really only this morning?* Then my mind began to wonder what he was doing now, with Her Royal Hiney.

For just a moment, I thought about trying to walk all the way to the camp store where I could call my Gramps to come and pick me up. I could just go home; pretend this horrid trip had never happened.

But I couldn't do that. To begin with, it would be extremely childish. Furthermore, I was lost. I had no idea where the camp store was located.

I walked a few more steps in silent misery, insects gnawing at my neck, chest aching and sore, throat parched . . . and I was pretty sure a blister was forming on my right heel. I was a mess. In fact, if I hadn't been such a mess, I might've noticed the woman in white a lot sooner.

She was walking—or rather, floating—along beside me, about an arm's length away.

I don't know how long she'd been there when I discovered her, but just as I acknowledged the misty coolness wafting toward me, she disappeared. All I saw was a fleeting glimpse of white from the corner of my eye, a chiffon scarf caught on a small breeze.

"Hey," I called out. "Come back. I won't hurt you . . ."

"Hurt me?" The voice was much more solid than I would've thought. And it had come from behind me.

I spun around.

"Why would I think you could hurt me? You're the one who looks like something the cat dragged in."

I couldn't believe my eyes.

Nora was standing in the middle of the trail, just a few yards behind me.

My mind whirled. Maybe it was her that I saw, not the woman in white.

"What are you doing?" I asked.

She put her hand on her hip and tipped her chin up. "I'm just on my way to the store."

Her voice had an edge to it that let me know she was aware that I was lost. How long had she been following me? Did she see me fall? Was she the thing in the brush?

I decided to pretend I wasn't lost, and then I would just go along with her to the store. I was certain I could find my way back to camp from there. No way was I going to tell her that the storeowner had said he didn't even know her.

"How long have you been following me?" So much for pretending everything is normal . . . my mouth always said whatever it wanted.

Nora laughed. "Ever since you ran off from your boyfriend and that thing that was growing out of his side."

"Growing out of . . . Oh, you mean Karla." I chuckled at the strange image in spite of myself. "Yeah, she was kind of attached, wasn't she?"

The other girl spluttered laughter, too. Then she turned around and started back down the trail, in the opposite direction.

I didn't know what to do. If I followed her, she would *probably* lead me to the store, but was it really in the complete opposite direction? Had I really been that turned around? Well, she was the native. She's already told me she knew these woods like the back of her hand . . . still, could I trust her? *Should I?*

"Hey," I called again. "Wait!" I jogged to catch up, my aching ribs and parched throat all but forgotten. The alternative was simply wandering around on my own the way I had been doing for the last couple of hours. I didn't really want to keep at it until darkness fell.

Nora hesitated long enough for me to catch her.

"Thanks." I was out of breath. "I hope you don't mind me walking back to the store with you. I – I was sort of upset when I took off. I didn't really watch where I was going."

"Yeah. No joke, Sherlock. I've been watching you flounder around like a fish out of water. That was some fall back there."

"You saw me when I got the wind knocked out of me?" That made me mad. "And you didn't even say anything?"

I guess the tone of my voice finally got to her. She looked at me for the first time since I'd caught up to her.

"Did it occur to you I might have been hurt?" My voice was getting louder, and scratchier, by the syllable. My head was really pounding now.

She still didn't say anything.

I flung my braid off my shoulder and faced her squarely. "I could hardly get my breath! Why didn't you come to help me? To at least see if anything was broken."

Nasty Nora *still* didn't answer. She just looked at me without expression. The she faced forward and went on. She knew I would follow. And really, what choice did I have?

8

*W*e walked along in silence. The only sounds I heard were those of the woodland creatures and our soft footsteps, which were pretty well muted by the path's intermittent covering of leaves and pine needles. I didn't attempt any more conversation, nor did she offer any.

I began to count steps, just to occupy my mind, and to see how many minutes it would take to get to where we were going. Jase and I had attempted to count the steps between our houses once, and we'd discovered that we *could* walk about 100 steps each minute, if we really tried. We never did find out how many steps were between our houses, though. There were far too many.

I also tried to watch for landmarks just in case she *wasn't* taking me back to the store. Unfortunately, to me, everything looked the same: green, and dappled with droplets of late afternoon sunshine raining down upon us through the tall pines.

We walked for ten minutes—that's 1,000 steps if you're counting—if I wasn't counting too fast, that is. I couldn't believe it was only that far, but we did take what appeared to be a couple of short cuts, little trails that I never would have noticed if Nora hadn't been leading me. And that made me wonder if I had accidentally taken one of those little side-trails in my head-long rush to get away from Karla. Maybe that's how I'd gotten so turned around.

A couple of times, I was certain someone was behind me again, but each time I turned my head to catch a glimpse, nothing was there. Once, I was certain I saw a blur of white from the corner of my eye, but it was too quick to say that it was *positively* the woman in white.

I wanted to ask Nora if she knew anything about the woman. I figured, since she actually lived around here, that she would know all about her, but I never got the chance. Nora stayed five or six steps ahead of me, as if to discourage talking. And even though I had no trouble keeping up with long-legged Jase on any given day—except if we were on our bikes—it was all I could do to keep Nora in sight.

A time or two, I was convinced myself she was actually trying to lose me. The suspicion that she was simply taking me deeper into the woods before disappearing again kept surfacing in my mind. I could easily imagine her just sitting back to watch and laugh as I tried to find my way out again.

Thankfully, that didn't happen. While I was ruminating, and counting my steps, we arrived. I looked up to see how far ahead she'd gotten, and there was the store. We had come out on one side of it. I could see the trail to our campsite just across the parking lot. I'd have to traverse Crybaby Bridge to get back to camp, but that was one of those proverbial bridges I would cross when I came to it.

"Nora?" I called her name, to thank her for saving my butt, but she was nowhere to be seen. She'd disappeared, just like I'd been afraid she would do.

I looked around for a house. She'd said she lived near the store, but there were no houses, only trails leading to other campsites. *Maybe "near" doesn't mean the same thing to her that it does to me. To her, near could mean a mile or more. It certainly didn't take her very long to get places.*

The store looked cool and inviting. I felt in my pockets. I had a five-dollar bill Gramps had given me, "just in case." I kept it in my mom's old leather coin purse in my back pocket. The little purse was flat and very old. I'd carried it since the day of her funeral so many years earlier. Gramps always made sure I had some money inside. Now, I was very thankful that he did.

I took a deep breath, pulled open the screen door, and stepped inside. The door was on one of those springs that made a metallic *screeee* when it was opened. The spring was so powerful; the door almost sprang right out of my hand once I was through.

I grabbed it before it could slam.

The interior of the place was dim and cool, just like I remembered. It appeared to be deserted. The humming of the bait tank, which was plugged into the wall to keep the water circulating, was the only sound I could hear.

"Hello?" I crossed to the cold box and pulled out a Dr. Pepper. The icy bottles clanked together musically. I looked around again.

From the back of the store, someone must have opened a door because I was suddenly treated to a thin slice of country music radio. I was pretty sure it was Hank Williams singing "Your Cheatin' Heart."

"Hello?" The Dr. Pepper bottle was sweating in my hand. I set it on the scarred wooden counter and wiped my palm on my shorts.

"Hey! Stevie-girl, right?"

His voice was loud and jovial. *How had I not heard him coming?* Such a big man, yet he moved so quietly.

"Ye-e-s." I tried not to stammer. "I – I'm camping with the

Lee family on the other side of the creek . . ." I don't know why I
was so rattled. He just surprised me. "I thought I would stop in
and get another Dr. Pepper. Ten, two, and four . . . you know . . ."
Oh, brother. How stupid I must sound, quoting TV commercials.

The proprietor chuckled. "I understand. Addicted to RC
Cola, myself." He patted his generous belly beneath the butcher's apron he wore, and I was reminded of the sign outside that
said he would clean and prepare fish, for a fee. "Need to cut out
the sodas according to the wife." He patted his middle again.
"She seems to think they aren't good for my girlish figger."

I giggled.

He rang up my purchase and I gave him my five-dollar bill. I
hated to give it up. I'd sort of counted on bringing it back home
with me, saving it to shop for Christmas gifts for Gramps and
Jase, but I knew that wouldn't happen now. Once you break a
bill, it seems as if it just disappears. I laughed inwardly. That was
something my Gramps often said when he had to pay for something with a five or a ten. He'd say, "Well, that's the beginning of
the end for that one!"

I must have been smiling because when the proprietor (his
name tag said BILL) counted my change back to me, he said,
"Glad to see you're having a good time on your campout."

That brought me back to the present. *Good time?* Could he
not tell I'd been through the wringer out there in the woods?
Did it not even show on my face, was I not bruised and bloody? I
felt bruised and bloody, but I hadn't actually bothered to check.
Maybe he was simply used to seeing sweaty, filthy kids here at
the camp store.

"Thanks," I replied as he produced a church key and popped
the top off my Dr. Pepper.

I heard the metal cap clink against others when he tossed it
into the cardboard box beneath the counter. "Now, don't forget

to bring that bottle back for your refund, next time you come in."

"Yes sir," I said, as I folded my four ones into a neat little packet that would fit back into my change purse. I added the coins to it as well, and then I slipped it back into my pocket. It made a much thicker bulge now.

"Tell the Lee's hello for me," the man said.

"I will." I raised one hand in a goodbye wave. Then I was out the door, slugging down that cold, fizzy, Dr. Pepper as if there were no tomorrow.

THAT WAS the best drink I'd ever had in my entire life. I downed it before I had even crossed the parking lot so I simply turned around and started back to the store to get my nickel refund. I didn't really want to carry an empty bottle back to camp anyway.

When I turned, I caught a bit of movement from the corner of my eye. Was it Nora? Or could it be the woman in white? I hurried toward the corner of the store where I'd seen the flash.

I thought I saw something toward the rear of the store, so I crept down the side of the building and peeked around the back corner.

The owner was just going back into the rear door. I guess he had already finished whatever chore I had interrupted when I went in the front door a few moments earlier. The flash of white must have been his butcher's apron.

I hated to interrupt him if he wasn't finished. I didn't really even want to interact with him again, but I couldn't stand the thought of not getting my nickel back. So I opened the front door and went back inside.

The screech of the screen was just the same as before.

Bill was coming down the center aisle.

When he got to the counter, I handed the bottle to him silently.

"You were thirsty, weren't you?" His voice held a note of glee. I noticed he was now holding a filet knife that I hadn't even noticed the first time. He must have laid it on the counter when he rang up my purchases a few moments earlier, and then he'd probably forgot to pick it back up after I left.

"Yes sir," I replied. "It was good." I couldn't help but respond to his jovial personality. He handed me my nickel and I headed back to the front door.

"See ya," he said.

This time, I just waved and kept going. All of a sudden, I was in a hurry to get back to camp. I had the awful feeling the Lee's might be getting frantic. What if they had somehow called my Gramps and told him I was lost? The skin on my scalp puckered at the thought of him thinking something had happened to me.

I put my feet into overdrive.

I never noticed the way the afternoon sun had begun to slip toward the western horizon. Nor did I notice the hulking shape of the bear nosing around the shed where Bill cleaned his customer's fish.

9

I was almost to the bridge, and slowing considerably, when I heard the tremendous crashing behind me. My entire body seized up much like the spring on the camp store door and I almost tripped as I craned my head around to see what was coming.

A black bear was loping toward me in a cloud of insect-ridden dust. Its fur wasn't shiny it just looked dirty. Even from a distance the bear's eyes looked too small for its huge head. As I watched, it stopped to smell the edge of the trail, testing my scent to see if I was worth pursuing.

Time slowed as I examined the animal.

I couldn't seem to take in the fact of a bear coming toward me. Hadn't Mr. Lee assured me there *were* no bears here?

I seemed to be in a state of disbelieving paralysis, still half-turned in the middle of the trail, my muscles poised to take flight, but my mind refusing to give the signal.

Suddenly, it lifted that impossibly long snout and peered through the gloom in my direction.

Run! My brain screamed. *Just run!*

Somehow my feet righted my unbalanced body and I *ran*. I

only knew I was crossing Crybaby Bridge because of the light *thwacking* sound my Keds made on the old wood.

Thwack thwack thwack thwack thwack thwack thwack and I was across.

The bear had started after me again, still at a lope as far as I could tell—I wasn't about to look back to make sure—but it paused at the entrance to the bridge.

I took advantage of its hesitation and dashed for the nearest tree with low growing branches. My sore chest was forgotten. My worry about the Lee's and Gramps was forgotten. Even my terror was forgotten now that I was on the move.

I wasn't positive climbing a tree was the right thing to do, but I was certain I couldn't outrun it on the trail—I hadn't even been able to keep up with Nasty Nora—but oh how I wished she were here *now*.

I launched myself at the lowest branch of a pine just as the bear made up its mind to cross the bridge. It acted almost confused, as if it didn't know whether to pursue me or turn around and go home.

I didn't wait for it to decide.

Up, up, up, I scrambled, the rough bark tearing at my skin.

The sound of thick black claws on the old wooden bridge served as an added incentive, spurring me higher and higher into the needles and branches. I had the idea that if I got up high enough, it wouldn't be able to see me.

I could feel pine tar trying to glue my palms to the trunk of the tree. My skin was bleeding in several places, lacerated by the sharp, scaly, bark.

The pine needles stabbed at me every inch of the way—as if they were on the side of the bear. My tank top and shorts offered very little protection.

But anything's better than becoming bear food.

I continued to scramble from branch to branch, listening

hard for the sound of claws on wood because when the sound of the claws stopped, that meant the bear was across the bridge.

For the life of me, I couldn't remember if grown bears climbed trees. I knew cubs did—I had a book about Smokey the Bear Cub—but it didn't really matter. I was in the tree now, with nowhere to go but up.

Suddenly, a deep *whuff* sounded directly below me as the bear destroyed my theory about not being seen.

I hugged the sticky trunk tightly as the bear swatted the base of my tree with its catcher's-mitt paws, nearly knocking me from my precarious perch. I clutched the trunk even tighter and pressed my whole body against it, including my face.

The bear *roared*. It seemed as if it had finally made up its mind about me and was determined to knock me down. That roar terrified me even worse than the baby doll walking into my tent.

It slammed the tree again.

Pine needles shivered down around me and my left foot slipped off the sticky branch. Luckily, I'd just taken a higher step with my right foot, and I yanked myself upward, gripping the rough trunk with all my might, grinding my face into the wavy bark, my eyes squenched firmly shut against reality.

Whuff!

The bear prepared to smack my tree again.

I opened my eyes and looked down. I couldn't help myself. The bear wasn't coming up. But neither had it gone away. As I watched, it pushed against the base of my tree almost *playfully*, as if testing the tree's strength.

In that tiny pocket of silence, I could hear the creek water lapping gently around the pillars of the old bridge.

The bear stopped pushing. It drew back its upper body and *smashed* the tree with both paws, its claws ripping through the bark and sending bits and pieces flying through the air.

I screamed.

I didn't know I *could* scream so loudly. The sound tore up out of my chest like a chain saw tearing through soft wood. I think I meant to scare the bear away. Janis Joplin would have been proud.

The bear *roared* again, peering up at me through the tatted separation of branches. It couldn't reach me. I'd gotten too high. The branches that held my teenage weight would not hold a grown bear, and it seemed to know that.

But its savage little eyes *saw* me anyway. They saw *into* me.

I think it saw my *fear*, or sensed it perhaps, and it knew I was no match for it, no matter how loudly I could scream. And then somehow the beady little eyes changed and I felt myself staring down into twin black holes of nothingness.

My hair stood up beneath my braid—I only *thought* I was terrified before—looking into that bear's savage gaze was like looking into an abyss, a place where nothing lived. For a moment, just an instant, I thought I was looking into the face of the woman in white. The one from my dream. In a place where there is no hope. No bargaining. No quarter. And as I stared down though the branches, into the eyes that were more like bottomless pits of despair, I found myself wondering if there was really a bear there at all. Or was it simply another type of phantom, one I'd never encountered before?

I snatched a pinecone and hurled it down.

It smacked the thing right between the eyes.

I hurled another and another and another as the bear snarled and whammed the tree with all its might. I kept the cones raining down on the bear's eyes and nose, finding the target every now and then until, suddenly, there were no more cones near me.

As soon as my onslaught ended, the bear roared and began to pound the tree again. Its claws made deep gashes in the wood, and I wondered if the tree would get so weak that the whole thing would finally break, tumbling me to the ground.

Panicked, I climbed higher, as high as I could—just a few more branches and I would be out of running room—but at least there were more pinecones here. I began to tear them off the branches—some were still green and wouldn't turn loose—so I fought them, twisting and yanking—

"Stevie!"

I turned my head. The sound of the bear tearing at my tree with its monstrous claws made it hard to tell if I'd really heard that or if—

"*Stevie!* Where are you?"

It was! That *was* Jase's voice.

"Up here!" I yelled. "I'm up here, in the tree!"

The sound of two voices must have confused the bear. It fell down on all fours and turned toward the new sound.

All at once, an outrageous clatter arose from the forest. It sounded as if an entire marching band—armed with metal drums—was coming through the woods.

The sounds grew louder and louder until I was almost ready to cover my ears and beg them to stop—but there was no way I was turning loose of that pine trunk, not even to cover my ears.

The bear looked up at me once—just a bear again—then it loped away, in the opposite direction of the cacophony coming through the trees.

I wanted to move, to alert Jase to my exact location, but I was unable to move.

I clung to the trunk as if it were the tree of life itself. Then I waited for whatever would happen next.

The metallic banging grew louder, and louder, and even louder, then it abruptly cut off.

I strained to see through my ladder of branches.

I almost cried with relief when I saw Jase standing in the

clearing holding a large cook pot in one hand and a wooden spoon in the other. His dad was beside him holding the lids to two pots. Leading the small troop was a park ranger with some sort of rifle and a walkie-talkie. They were standing back to back in a semi-circle, peering out into the gloom. Mr. Lee was also carrying a large flashlight.

"Jase!" I croaked. "Up here . . ." I shook some branches and tossed down one of my last pinecones. "Where's the bear?" My voice was little more than a hoarse whisper. I had no way of knowing how long I'd been screaming.

Jase ran to the base of my tree. He let out a low whistle through his teeth. "Bear alright," he said to the ranger. "Look." He placed his hand over the six-inch claw marks on the tree trunk. Then he gazed up to my roost. I was clinging to the trunk like a terrified monkey.

I was so glad to see all that white-blond hair shining through the murky gloom.

"You okay, Stevie-girl?" That was Mr. Lee's voice.

I nodded. Then I realized he couldn't see me. "I'm okay," I squawked. I cleared my throat and tried to force my voice to be louder. "Where's the bear?" I was so afraid it was going to reappear out of the gloom and attack them before the ranger could even raise the gun.

"It's gone, honey," the ranger called. "We scared it away."

Mr. Lee shined the big flashlight all around the clearing and into the trees as far as the light would go. "It's safe, Stevie." His voice was comforting. "Come on down."

I clasped the remaining pinecones in the crook of one arm, and tried to make my feet lower me to the branch below. But they would not move.

"I, um, I don't think I can . . ." I felt a sob building in my sore throat.

Jase was below me before I even realized he'd started to

climb. "Give me your hand," he said. His voice was calm, but with an edge to it like a serrated steak knife.

He's mad at me, I thought. I felt like such a fool, causing everyone so much trouble. A sob escaped me and then Jase was there. He didn't even say anything, he just came up and up until he was high enough to wrap his long arms around my tree and around me. We were anchored there for some time while I buried my face into the crook of my own arm and cried. "I'm sorry," I said at last.

"You? I'm the one who should be sorry. It's my fault you got chased up a tree by a bear." He laughed darkly. "I followed you, but it was as if you'd disappeared. Your old friend is something else, isn't she?"

I nodded, not trusting my voice. I'd almost forgotten about Karla.

"Come on." He began to ease his way back down, never letting go of some part of me. "I've got you," he promised. Then he guided my feet to the lower branches, one by one, until we were safely on the ground.

It was downright embarrassing, the way the calves of my legs trembled as he guided my feet down to each lower branch. My legs acted as if I had run a marathon.

Mr. Lee and the ranger were standing patiently. The ranger wrapped me in a small poncho, even though I didn't think I was cold. "Don't want you going into shock," he said.

I didn't think *that* was possible. Not now.

I accepted the poncho, though. It made me feel safer to wrap it around my bare shoulders.

"Looks like you encountered the only bear to visit this camp in twenty years," the ranger said. "Bill called me on the radio right after you left the store. Said he was pretty sure a bear had been at his fish shack. Then he told us you had been there only a few minutes earlier."

I felt my eyes widen as he spoke.

"He was sure worried about you," the ranger continued. "We were awful glad when we heard you screaming."

"But scared . . . " Jase added, hugging me through the poncho. I was tucked up against his side, his arm around my shoulders. "I never heard you sound like that—I thought the bear had you—then we realized what you were saying."

"Saying?" I was puzzled. I only remembered screaming.

Jase looked down at me. "You were screaming 'get out of here, get out of here you ugly beast!'" He hugged me again, chuckling good naturedly.

"I was terrified," I admitted. "I don't remember yelling those words, or any words for that matter."

Jase laughed softly. "You didn't sound scared. You just sounded mad. Furious."

So I guess it was a bear I'd been seeing all along. I felt better, and worse. Then a thought occurred to me. Nora! Could she have been the one yelling at the bear? Wouldn't I have remembered if I were the one yelling?

"What about Nora?" My voice was as rough as the pine bark.

"Who?" The ranger asked.

"Nora, the girl who lives near the camp store."

The park ranger shook his head. "No one lives near the camp store except for Bill. And it couldn't be any of his kids. They're all grown. None of them live near here that I know of . . ."

I felt Jase's grip tighten around my shoulders. I knew what he was thinking. Nora might be a phantom, too.

"I – I guess I heard her wrong. She must've said she was *camping* near the store." I knew that wasn't what she'd said, and Jase knew it, too. But there are some times when it's best *not* to tell everything you know. Besides, at that moment, Nora was the least of my worries.

10

_W_hen we got back to camp, Mrs. Lee was sitting inside the parked car for safety. The ranger said everyone had to clear out on account of the bear, but of course the Lees couldn't go until I was found. The ranger had told us they would try to tranquilize the bear and relocate it to the mountains since it hadn't hurt anyone yet. But first, he would have to make certain all the campers were safely out of the park.

Then I noticed another vehicle there, too. It was a blue station wagon with two people sitting inside.

When we got close enough for the people in the cars to see us, Karla climbed out of the station wagon and strolled into the lake. Her yellow bikini glowed in the last meager rays of the sun. In the clearing, it wasn't quite as dark as it had been in the woods.

I looked down at my legs sticking out of the poncho. They were scratched and bleeding in a dozen places, but the worst part was the sticky black pine tar. It was smeared here and there all over my body, and my clothes.

Without a word, I handed the ranger his poncho and waded

into the lake, too. I would help pack up later; right now, I wanted this sticky mess *off!*

I grabbed handfuls of mud off the lake bottom and scrubbed at my palms, arms, and legs. It stung in the cuts, but not much. Mostly, it felt good. I sensed Karla wading back out, but I didn't turn. As far as I was concerned, she no longer existed. I'd wasted enough time missing her and watching for her father on the nightly news, and . . . *if I kept thinking like this, I would soon be blubbering.* I scrubbed even harder, determined to get all traces of my ordeal in the tree off me before climbing back into the car for the long ride home. I wasn't sure who had really ruined the trip: Karla, the bear, or *me.*

Just as I thought her name, I heard her voice.

I couldn't help it; I looked up.

There she was, yellow bikini like a spotlight in the gloaming. And she was whispering something into Jase's ear. She had him pulled down to her level with one hand on his shoulder—again! *Was she pointing at me?*

My blood shot through my veins right up to my face and I literally saw a red film steal across my vision. *What happened to the girl I used to know?*

I stomped out of the shallows, my feet sending sprays of water into the air with each determined step. For a second, I concentrated on making the water splash higher and higher— and then I was there, standing in front of my oldest, and I thought, dearest, friend.

"Glad to see you were so worried about me." I almost choked on the words when she grabbed another handful of Jase's shirt and pulled him down again.

As I watched, she whispered something else into his ear and I saw Jase's face redden. He began to straighten up and pull away at the same time and I heard the tail end of Karla's sentence, " . . . just a little girl. Not like me, I know how to treat a boy."

"A little girl, huh?" My voice was loud, but shaky. I squeezed the water from my braid and looked right at her. "We're the same age, Karla."

She looked me up and down. Water was dripping from my cutoffs and my red tank top was plastered to my body like a second skin. "You're just a kid, though. You know what I mean." One corner of her mouth twitched cruelly, as if she were sparing my feelings by not saying more.

"What's wrong with you, Karla? I thought you were my best friend." *Now the tears would begin.* I snuffled. "Guess I was wrong about that. Guess I was just *convenient* all those years, living on the same street and all."

Karla's face was blank. She appeared to have no idea what I was talking about. And she was still holding onto Jase's shirt as if he were some sort of anchor.

With as much dignity as I could muster, I strode past them toward the tents. I wanted some dry clothes and a dark corner.

"Stevie!"

I turned just as Jase shook himself loose.

"Wait up." He flipped his hair off his forehead and loped toward me. "I'll go with you."

Karla reached for her towel. She'd hung it over a bush that sported a trio of leaves on each reddish stem. I opened my mouth to warn her, "Don't touch! That's poison ivy!" But it was too late. She had grabbed her towel, dragged it all across the top of the bush, and was vigorously scrubbing at her face and neck. She was even standing with several of the branches brushing her bare legs.

Until now, I had never even noticed the poison plant growing this close to the campsite.

I think my mouth was hanging open.

Beside me, I heard Jase snicker.

"Is that what I think it is?" I whispered.

He nodded. "Looks like John Lennon was right about Instant Karma."

I turned and hurried toward the tent, giggles erupting through the fingers covering my mouth. I was still dripping wet and very hurt, but I felt better. Karla was about to be knocked off her high horse in a very public, very painful way.

Jase turned back. "Hey, Karla . . . you might want to stop by the camp store for some Calamine Lotion on your way out." His voice wasn't that loud, but in the woodsy clearing, it carried.

I glanced back in time to see Karla turn, infected towel in hand. "Why?"

Jase casually waved his hand toward the low-growing bush. "That plant you're standing in is poison ivy."

Karla looked down, took two giant steps backward—as if she were playing *Mother May I?*—and then looked at the towel in her hands.

"Gross!" she flung the towel to the ground and immediately began to scratch at her arms and legs, but I thought it was just reflex. I didn't think it could have affected her that quickly. Besides, it was her face that was going to take the brunt of the poison—she had plunged both hands into the bush when she grabbed up her towel—and then she'd rubbed the towel all over her face.

I had a dark moment when I pictured, in my mind, what poison ivy blisters might look like if they got into her eyes. It would be awful. *Did I care?* I had to think about that for a moment. *I was almost snack-food for a bear because of her.*

Without another thought, I ducked into the tent I'd shared with Mrs. Lee. She had already rolled up our sleeping bags and tied them neatly. My extra clothes were in my duffle in the corner.

"You okay?" Jase asked, standing just outside the tent flap.

"I'm all right." My voice was much better now that I'd seen Karla scrub herself with poison ivy.

"Stevie? Stevie-girl?" That sounded like Karla's mom.

I peeked out. "Yes, ma'am?" I hoped she wasn't about to scold me for not warning Karla about the plant.

Instead, she patted my cheek lightly. I only had my head stuck out through the tent flap.

Jase looked away. "I'll help Dad finish loading the car," he said.

Stepping outside, I faced her mom squarely. I wasn't really in the mood for a lecture, so I was completely surprised when she pulled me to her chest in a fierce hug. "I'm so sorry," she whispered. Her voice sounded a little chokey, too.

"Why?" The word slipped out. I was confused. She hadn't done anything to me.

She turned me loose and stepped back. "For the way Karla has been acting. I know that's why you took off. I would have, too, if I'd been in your shoes. I had no idea she would act this way . . . I thought she would be thrilled to see you." She looked down, examined her thumbnail. "I think her attitude might be partly my fault. You see I've been sort of holding you up as a shining example of how she should act. In fact, I was hoping she might want to go home with you for a few days, or invite you to go with us. You know, the way you girls used to spend whole weekends together, and then beg for more . . ."

I nodded slowly. What was she trying to say?

The older woman sighed and glanced toward Karla who had rushed back into the water and, in an odd imitation of me, was now scrubbing at her skin with handfuls of mud. "She's changed so much." Her eyes found mine, and for the first time, she really looked at me. I was reminded of the bear, or rather, the feeling I'd gotten when the bear looked into my eyes, as if there were very little hope residing there.

"The California move was devastating for her," she said. "She missed you terribly, moping around, never leaving the house."

Looks like she recovered, I thought. But I didn't say anything.

"I'm afraid I pushed her to make new friends," she continued. "Any friends." She bit her lip. "And then when she chose the wrong ones, I compared them all to you. I was so desperate for her to be happy again, I'm afraid I messed everything up." She glanced at her daughter again. "Now, I don't even know her."

I tried to let myself feel sorry for her, or even for Karla. But the image of the bear kept popping into my head. The sounds it made. The way the pine tree shook and showered me with needles each time the bear smacked it.

"I'm sorry," I said at last. "I wish sh—" I was going to say I wish she was still the same, but that seemed cruel. Instead I said, "I wish *you* all the best." I ducked back into the tent and began to peel off my wet clothes, hoping against hope that she wouldn't pull the tent flap open and follow me.

I wanted to take a shower. Even after I'd shed my clothes and dried myself with my towel, I still felt dirty. The pine tar had gone right through my tank top—I'd been hugging the tree that hard. As I scrubbed at the ugly smears, I found myself in tears, shaking like one of the pine needles just before it fell.

"Stevie?" Jase was back.

I wiped at my face with the now-sticky towel, and cleared my throat, willing my voice to sound somewhat normal. "Be out in a minute," I said.

"No hurry." His voice sounded strained, too. Probably trying to keep Karla from hearing him—one touch and he'd be infected with the poison ivy oil, too.

I giggled wetly, my tears still hovering in the back of my

throat. I was thinking of how Karla was going to look in that bikini tomorrow.

"What's so funny?" Jase stage-whispered.

I yanked the zipper up on a clean pair of cutoffs, pulled my clean tee shirt over my head, and stepped out. "Karla will be tomorrow," I said.

Jase snorted, then leaned down and rubbed at a spot on my nose. "You're still covered with goo . . ."

That reminded me of the first time I had met the phantom pilot. We'd been at Jase's house, in the back field—and he'd been about to show me the place where the plane had crashed—when gray balls of jelly-goo began to rain down on us from the sky.

"Does it look like the jelly rain the phantom pilot pelted us with?" I asked, gently pushing his hand away.

Jase smiled and chucked me under the chin. "Almost." He rubbed at another spot on my cheek. "But this is a lot harder to get off."

I headed down the trail. Karla was nowhere in sight. I didn't even see her mom anywhere. Mr. and Mrs. Lee were taking down the other tent.

"Where you going?" Jase caught up with me in two steps.

"I'm going to the bathroom to see what you keep trying to rub off." I elbowed him in the ribs, gently.

He took hold of my arm. "Did you forget there's a bear on the loose?"

Actually, I had forgotten. Oh, not about the bear itself. I was pretty certain the image of those unblinking little eyes would live in my memory forever—but it already seemed as if it had happened to someone else.

"Yeah," I laughed. "I had forgotten, sort of." I stopped in my tracks. "But I really would like to go and clean up a little better."

Jase just shook his head. "Attacked and almost eaten, and

already she forgets." He turned me to face him. "Now tell me you aren't the brave one."

His voice had grown disturbingly soft as he leaned toward me. "I'm not." I whispered. "Not even."

He bonked his forehead to mine. "I'm sorry I let you down."

His eyes were closed, his forehead resting on mine. For a moment I wondered if his skin was stuck to me with a blob of pine tar. A giggle bubbled up in my throat at the ridiculous thought.

"It wasn't your fault," I said. "If I was really brave, I would've clobbered her instead of running off like that." I stuck the tip of my braid in my mouth. I felt so silly, admitting that I'd let Karla get the best of me just by flirting with Jase. But of course it wasn't only the flirting . . . it was the fact that she was supposed to be glad to see *me*, her best friend. Instead, she brushed me aside like a pesky insect and went straight for Jase, my new best friend. But it was all after-the-fact, now.

"Yeah," he agreed. "You should have."

I opened my eyes again. His green ones were staring straight into mine.

He smiled. "Clobbered her, I mean. With a stick. A big one."

I did giggle then. I couldn't help it. "I will, next time."

Jase tipped his head back and guffawed. Sure enough, there was a dot of sticky tar on his forehead.

I started toward the bathroom once more. "Surely old Mr. Bear is long gone by now," I said. But I was watching the woods very carefully. It just didn't seem real anymore. Everything that had happened seemed surreal, as if I'd dreamed it. Just another bad dream.

THE SUN WAS COMPLETELY DOWN, all that was left to light the night were the scattered rays glowing upward from the horizon.

I could see the outdoor light that signified the public bathrooms. It was only a few more yards.

"Hey," Jase caught me again. This time, when he turned me around, he didn't let go of my elbow.

I looked up at his face. He wasn't smiling anymore.

"There won't be a next time." His voice was serious.

"No?" I didn't know what he was getting at.

He smoothed the heavy chunk of blond hair off his forehead with his free hand. "Never." He crooked his forefinger under my chin and made me look into his eyes. "You're my best friend, Stevie-girl. Have been since the day you clobbered *me* with a loaf of bread." He smiled softly, just a quirk of his lip.

I tried to look away. The intensity of his gaze made me uncomfortable.

He pulled my face back toward his. "And you always will be. No matter what."

Something loosened up in my chest. It felt like the loosening of a shoelace that's been tied too tightly and suddenly gives a bit.

"Okay." My voice was so small I wasn't sure he could hear me. But I guess he did. He pulled me to his chest and kissed the top of my sticky head.

From the corner of my eye, I could see the woman in white staring at us from the edge of the forest.

When I opened my mouth to tell Jase, she faded away like mist on a sunny day.

11

I took off toward the spot where I'd seen the woman. Jase tightened his grip on my arm, pulling me back.

"Where you going? The bathrooms are this way." He tried to steer me toward the path.

I shook myself free. "The woman in white," I said. "She was watching us."

Jase tightened his grip even more. "No, Stevie." His voice was as unfathomable as the night. "There's a fine line between brave and foolish."

I stopped. "But we need to see her before we have to leave. We haven't helped her at all." In the other two cases of phantoms, we'd been able to figure out what they wanted and help them cross over to the other side. At least I was pretty certain we'd done that. We hadn't seen them anymore. Even Jase's ghost dog, Lady, had gone over.

Jase shook his head. "I'll walk with you and stand outside the restroom while you clean up . . . but I won't let you go back into the forest. I'm not even sure we should be standing here on the trail." His face was turned away, half-hidden by shadow. "I saw that bear, too," he said. "Remember?"

We both glanced around nervously. "You're right." I looked toward the bathrooms longingly. "I don't think we should go any further." The thought of Jase standing outside the little lighted building, exposed to the creatures of the night just so I could peel a little sap off my face, that didn't seem so important anymore.

"C'mon." I turned around. "Let's just get back to camp as quickly as possible. You're right. We can't save 'em all."

"Now you're talking," he agreed.

Before I knew it, we were practically racing.

It took only minutes to disassemble the girls' tent and stow it in the trunk with the other tent and supplies. Then we all climbed in and Mr. Lee started the engine. "You're friend's mom said to tell you they would probably catch up with you in Cross-roads in the next few days." He glanced at me in the rearview mirror. "I nodded. *What a relief not to have to deal with them anymore.*

"Dad?"

Mr. Lee looked at Jase in the mirror. "What is it, son?"

"Could we stop by the restrooms before we head out?" He patted my hand, which was lying on the seat between us.

"Of course," he answered. "But if you don't mind, I'll go in and check them out before you kids go inside."

I smiled and squeezed Jase's fingers in thanks.

"Sounds like a good deal," he replied.

MR. AND MRS. LEE both inspected the bathrooms, and when they were deemed safe and bear free, they motioned for us to come on in.

I was glad Mrs. Lee was with me this time. I'd had enough phantom-encounters for this trip. If we couldn't help the woman in white, then I was ready to be done with her. The more I thought of it, the more I came to believe that she might have been the reason the bear chased me. Phantoms can do strange things—the phantom pilot threw farm implements at us and caused the jelly rain to fall—who's to say one of them couldn't call down a bear if necessary?

After I scrubbed my sticky spots with soap and paper towels, we were all very surprised when we got back to the car and found the park ranger waiting for us.

"The bear was spotted by one of the other officers," he said, removing his ranger hat and holding it between his hands. "She is moving back toward the mountains where she probably has a den with a cub or two inside. I just wanted to check and make sure you folks are okay." He looked directly at me. "Especially you, young lady. You had quite a scare."

"I'm okay," I said. If he only knew some of the scares I'd had while I'd been here. But he was right, the bear was the worst.

"Thank you for checking on us," Mr. Lee said. "Wonder what made a mama bear leave her cubs and come all the way down here . . ."

The ranger shook his head. "It's a bit of a mystery to us, too." A sheepish grin creased his pleasant face and I got a sudden image of Ranger Smith from the Yogi Bear cartoons. It made me giggle.

Mr. Lee beamed. "Good news, isn't it, Stevie-girl?"

I nodded, swallowing my giggles behind my hand. "Very good news."

Mr. Lee and the ranger shook hands and we all piled back into the car.

"Who's up for celebration ice cream?" he asked.

The three of us, even Mrs. Lee, raised our hands and shouted, "Me, me, me!"

Mr. Lee slapped the gearshift into drive and away we went.

"To the camp store!" he shouted. "Damn the torpedoes, full speed ahead!"

I saw Mrs. Lee reach over and swat her husband's knee once, sharply, as if admonishing him for the bad word.

But I knew it was just a quote from the Civil War. And when something is a quote from someone else, it doesn't count if you say it. At least, I think that's how it works, besides, I appreciated his enthusiasm. It was a relief to know the bear really was gone —and that it had actually been just a bear after all.

I leaned back in the seat, thankful for the darkness. What an awful day it had been. But it was already beginning to seem like a lifetime ago. I think I was simply exhausted.

Thankfully, it took only a few minutes to get to the store. As we exited the car, we were treated to a show of heat lightning that crackled soundlessly in the distance.

We trooped inside, single file.

"Hope that isn't headed this way," Mrs. Lee remarked to Bill, the storeowner.

The big man jerked a thumb over his shoulder. A small black radio sat behind him on the counter. "Weather radio," he said. "I get alerts if a storm is coming."

My skin crinkled the same way it did when the woman in white was behind us in the woods. "How often do you get alerts?" I asked.

Bill laughed. "None lately. There's nothing for you to worry about." He smiled kindly. "You've had enough excitement for one trip. I sure was concerned about you."

"Thank you for helping them find me," I said. His words made me feel better. I recalled the feeling I got in the forest that someone was watching over me. Maybe that someone had been Bill.

It was also nice to know Bill and his radio were on guard in case of bad weather. We had a long drive in front of us, and I wasn't positive, but I thought we were going to be driving directly toward the lightning.

No one else seemed worried.

To celebrate the good news about the bear, the four of us chose Nutty Buddy Ice Cream cones, and Mrs. Lee suggested we eat them in the parking lot before they melted. I knew she was afraid we would make a mess in the car, and she was right. I'd never had one that didn't shed at least some of its chocolate and nuts before I was through.

I sat on the low iron rail that ran across the front of the parking lot. Jase and his dad leaned against the car, and Mrs. Lee sat on the bumper.

We didn't talk much. We were all intent upon finishing our treats with the least amount of waste. No one wanted to lose so much as a single peanut, they were that good.

As we sat there, chomping our treats in companionable silence, a nice, new Oldsmobile pulled into the lot, and a little old man about half the size of Mr. Lee climbed out. He touched the brim of his hat—I think it was the kind known as a fedora—and said "Ma'am," to Mrs. Lee. Then he opened the door and disappeared into the store.

We heard Bill's hearty voice. "Why, Cletus Brown! What brings you all the way out here?"

I could picture the two of them shaking hands the way old friends do—clapping each other on the shoulders as their hands met.

We couldn't hear Cletus's reply, but we could easily hear everything that Bill said. His voice was like Jase's, it just naturally carried.

"Is that right?" he said. "After all these years?"

That got my curiosity up. I stuffed the pointed end of the Nutty Buddy in my mouth and made it disappear. Then I said, "Think I'll get a quick drink."

I hurried inside. There was a cold water fountain near the ice cream freezer. For some reason, ice cream really does make me thirsty. Fortunately, the fountain was close enough to the two men that I could hear every word they said.

Maybe I was being nosy, eavesdropping, but at the same time, I felt an itch to encounter someone who seemed to have been around for a while.

Guess I hadn't completely given up on the idea of helping the woman in white, after all.

"What's up?" Jase asked. He was standing directly behind me. I'd been so intent on listening, I hadn't even heard him come in.

Bill and Cletus were sitting at a little booth near the back of the store.

"Cletus used to own this place," I whispered. I held my finger to my lips and motioned for Jase to get a drink, too. I wanted an excuse to stay and listen some more.

Cletus told Bill that someone named Stanley had passed away and his daughter was in town for the funeral.

I nudged Jase to keep drinking so I could hear more.

"First time she's been back," he said. "Not sure if she knows, or not."

Now my curiosity was *really* piqued.

I sidled up to the post card display as if I were looking for one to buy. Turning the wire rack slowly, I continued to eavesdrop.

"Surely old Stan told her the history. She was just an infant, but he had to know she'd find out someday . . ."

The word infant nearly burned my ears. My hand stopped twirling the rack. I looked at Jase. He was looking back at me, still bent over the water fountain, cold dribbles clinging to his chin.

I raised my eyebrows in a questioning gesture. *Are you hearing this?*

He nodded once.

I didn't know what to do. It was becoming obvious that Jase and I were simply killing time.

The front door opened—*scree*—and Jase's dad called out, "You kids about ready to go?"

"Coming, Dad." Jase wiped his chin with the back of his hand.

I left the card rack and started after Jase, but the next words froze me in my tracks.

"If only Nora hadn't fallen . . ."

That was Cletus.

I was as still as stone, listening. Mr. Lee's mouth was open as if he was about to ask us to hurry, but even he had heard the name Nora.

We all waited to see what Bill would say.

"That's right, the girl's name *was* Nora, wasn't it?"

I heard him push himself up from the booth. It made a little scraping sound on the concrete floor.

"What's that been, fifty, sixty years ago?"

"Something like that," Cletus replied. His bench scraped, too. "I went to Stan's funeral this afternoon. Paid my condolences to Lillian." He stroked his chin thoughtfully. "You know, he and his wife moved to Dallas after they adopted her. Guess he wanted her to bring him back here to be buried. His wife died years ago—but she wasn't a local girl—don't know where she's buried. Do folks still talk about the flood?"

Bill grunted. "They do. In fact, they say they can still hear the baby under the bridge. Not me. I don't even venture down that way if I can help it."

I turned. I couldn't help myself. "I thought you'd never heard of Nora." I didn't mean to sound accusing, especially not to an adult, but sometimes my mouth spoke before my brain even knew it was open.

Bill looked up as if he'd forgotten all about us. "Well, honey, the Nora we're talking about has been gone almost sixty years. She drowned in Stutter Creek back in 1911. Big flood that year. Drowned trying to save a little baby named Lillian. If only she hadn't tripped." He looked at Cletus for confirmation.

"Yep," the old man agreed. "That's when the baby flew out of her grasp. The ground was solid mud and the water was rising . . . That's the story I heard anyhow."

"Oh." My hands were clenched so tightly my nails were digging into my palms. "How awful. Was Lillian her baby?"

Cletus spoke up then. "Oh no, Nora was just a girl." He looked me over carefully. "She was about your caliber. Good family." He placed his hat back on his head in preparation for leaving. "Knew the whole bunch. Nearly killed 'em when she drowned. Nearly did 'em in." He shook his grizzled old head sadly.

"I'm sorry," I replied. And I really was. But I had to probe a bit further. "So who *was* the baby's mother?"

Cletus and Bill looked at each other.

"Guess it doesn't matter now," Bill said. He walked around the counter and busied himself with straightening the packs of gum near the register. His voice was sort of bland when he spoke. "Nora was babysitting when a flash flood took everyone by surprise. The baby's mama was a woman named Wanda. She was a nurse down at the county hospital."

Cletus took up the story, "She had to work late that night. Nora offered to watch little Lillian—she was only a year old. Just learning to toddle." He seemed to be thinking back. "Wanda dropped the baby off at Nora's place. Her folks had a big old farmhouse right near here, but they weren't home yet, either.

Nobody home but Nora. That wasn't unusual. Kids were much more independent then . . ."

"What happened?" I saw Jase's mom step inside to see what was taking so long.

Cletus was quite firmly back in the past, now. "I lived with my folks on the other side of the lake." He wiped a broad thumb under one eye. "Nora and I used to catch crawfish in the creek when the water was low." When he said creek, it sounded more like "crick." His voice grew quieter. "She'd be my age now." He wiped his eyes again. "We could hear her calling for Lillian during the flood. All the way across the lake, we could hear her. Once, I thought I heard Wanda calling for her, too. But that was hard to tell. By then my family was struggling to get to higher ground. Once, I thought I heard the baby cry out—but I couldn't tell if the little thing was calling Wanda or Mama. They sort of sounded the same—"

"*Wahhmahh*?" I said the word aloud without thinking.

Cletus's head jerked up. It was obvious he'd forgotten I was there. "You've heard her?"

I nodded. "Several times." Taking a deep breath, I plunged ahead. "Saw her, too. Nora, I mean." I glanced at Jase to see if he was going to try and stop me from telling, but his face was impassive. "She dropped a baby doll in the water and it floated under the bridge and got tangled in some tree branches and stuff."

Cletus stumbled back to the little booth and sat down heavily.

The front door screen wailed again, and a petite woman with reddish-gray hair stepped inside. "Cletus," she called. "Is that you? I thought that was your car outside."

The older man brushed his hand across his face and stood once more. "Lillian? Come and meet these kids. They've got quite a story to tell . . ."

My eyes felt like they would pop right out of my head. *"Lillian?"* I looked to Cletus to see if this was the same woman we'd just been discussing. *Could she be the baby? But didn't the baby drown?*

Introductions were made all around, and then Lillian was given the seat of honor at the little booth. We quickly learned that she was in the town of Stutter Creek, just a few miles down the road, to attend the funeral of the man who had adopted her when she was just a little over one year old. He was the man who had pulled her from the creek the day after it flooded and drowned poor Nora and Wanda, her mother. Come to find out, Wanda had rushed home from the hospital when she heard about the flood, and dove right into the swollen creek—dove right off the bridge Bill said—looking for little Lillian.

"But I only found all this out two weeks ago when my father was certain he wasn't going to last much longer. He'd been battling the cancer for a long time." Lillian dabbed at her eyes with an embroidered handkerchief. "Oh, I knew I was adopted, that was never a secret." She smiled sadly. "But I never knew I was the infamous baby of Crybaby Bridge. Not until he was on his deathbed. That's when he told me how he'd pulled me from the pile of debris that had washed up on shore after the rain abated." She hiccupped or sobbed, I couldn't tell which. Then she continued. "Two people died trying to save me—my babysitter and my own mother. I can't understand why they died and I lived." She was quiet for a moment. "I think that's what my adoptive father was trying to spare me from. Knowing they died trying to save me. That's why I had to come back."

I released the breath I'd been holding. "Do you want to go out to the bridge?"

Lillian stood and grasped the back of the chair for support. "I think that's what I came here for." Her smile was sad. "I think I have to."

12

$\mathcal{J}$ase's parents looked at us as if we'd all grown enormous purple horns, but they went along. In fact, Bill gave us three big flashlights and we took off down the trail in a loose-knit group. All except for Bill. Just as he'd said earlier, he never went near the bridge. Not if he could avoid it.

Jase and I were leading the way, with Lillian and Cletus in the middle, and Mr. and Mrs. Lee acting as caboose.

When the first fat raindrops began to fall, we looked at each other apprehensively. I swiped a drop off my cheek, certain I'd been bombed by a night bird or something, but no. It wasn't bird poo or anything else; it was rain.

A huge bang of thunder turned our apprehensive expressions into grimaces of disbelief. The stroke of lightning that split the sky lit us up as surely as if we'd been standing inside a light bulb. Then it began to pour.

Within moments, our clothes were drenched and the red-dirt trail became a river of mud. I thought of Nora running down the trail with a baby in her arms.

"This isn't right!" I yelled.

Jase cupped his hand around his ear to indicate that he couldn't hear me. The wind had picked up; it was lashing us from the side as if it wanted to knock us off our feet. When there was a brief lull in the wind, the sheet of rain fell straight down in front of us like a thick silver curtain.

At times, I couldn't see *anything,* then the rain would momentarily slow, and the world would swim into view again.

Jase grabbed my hand. The flashlights were very little help.

All at once, the bridge loomed out of the storm like a bad dream.

The roar of the wind intensified and we heard a deep grinding noise. It was the sound of the old bridge straining against the weather. I wondered if Bill's radio had squawked out an alert yet.

"Flash flood!" Lillian cried.

We all looked downstream.

A wall of muddy red water boiled toward us out of the darkness. It wasn't stuttering and hiccupping along the way it usually did, this new version of the creek was on a mission to destroy everything in its path.

"It is a flood!" Cletus yelled.

The grinding noise grew louder as tree limbs and other debris clotted up around the bridge's wooden supports. Whole pieces of lumber, parts of a shed, even a roof, joined the tangled mess pounding against the bridge.

"Look!" I pointed to the opposite bank. A spear of lightning lit the scene and Wanda, the woman in white, appeared to part the rain with the ghostly brilliance of her nurse's uniform.

Dark hair plastered to her head, she floated onto the bridge. Her feet were invisible, shrouded in the violent mist caused by the hard raindrops hitting the bridge and bouncing back up around her ankles. She climbed onto the rails and peered into the roiling water, preparing to dive.

"Mama?" That was Lillian. Even though we could barely hear her, I could detect the strained disbelief in her voice. She shook free of Cletus and Mrs. Lee's hands and began to run. "Mama!" she yelled, her feet slip and sliding in the mud.

I held my breath and waited for the sound of her dress shoes on the wooden bridge. But the rain was too loud. *Had I really heard the sound of bear claws on that same wood only a few hours earlier? Could it be?* I squeezed Jase's hand solidly, to reassure myself that this was happening.

Then her shoes hit the wood and the rain stopped as if someone had thrown a giant rain-switch somewhere. The sound of her heels clacking on the bridge was amplified by the sudden silence.

Wait! I wanted to say. *Be careful!* But I had no time for any of that because in the space of a heartbeat, we heard a *c-r-a-a-c-k* as one of the supports broke and the far end of the bridge suddenly canted downward and to the left.

Wanda disappeared. Lillian fell to her knees and grabbed the railing in panic. It was as if the swollen creek was determined to claim the treasure it had been denied so many years earlier.

Jase took off toward the bridge, but his feet went right out from under him and he landed on his back with a bone-jarring thud. Mr. Lee and Cletus rushed forward as Jase did his best to push himself to his feet.

The rain came down again in *torrents*. The whole bridge scene disappeared from sight and I was certain Lillian had been washed away. *How could she possibly hold on in such a deluge?*

Mr. Lee was shaking his big flashlight back and forth. It had stopped working completely.

Cletus moved forward slowly, hands stretched out in front of him like a blind man. I was afraid he would walk right off into the water. It was impossible to tell where the bridge was, or if it was still there.

The howling wind grew even stronger. Pine needles and twigs flew through the air, smashed from the trees by the force of the rain.

A quick figure with bright blond hair flashed past me.

"Nora!" I cried. "Help them!"

The girl never slowed.

Huddled on the bank behind Cletus, we peered into the driving rain as Nora dashed into the maelstrom and disappeared.

"Wahhh*mahhh*."

We all heard it. At least I think we did. Our heads turned toward the raging water, away from the bridge. A tiny pink form shot out from under the place where the bridge should have been. It was quickly washed downstream and out of sight.

In a few moments, I realized I no longer had to strain to see through the storm. The rain was abating.

The six of us leaned forward as if we were one. The smell of the flooded creek mixed with the scent of pine and something that reminded me of a wet campfire. I was surprised to see that the bridge was still there. It was listing badly, but it wasn't gone.

Where was Lillian?

"*Wahhhmahhh.*" The sound floated to us on the moist air.

Lillian was standing on the opposite end of the shaky bridge. She was still grasping the rail with one hand. On either side of her stood a figure. One was small, with bright blond hair. The other was taller, with dark hair and a white uniform dress that glowed in the moonlight.

The clouds continued to scud away as the storm moved on.

The creek had calmed. It was very high, but it no longer lunged at the bridge or tried to climb out of its own banks.

As we watched, Nora handed the crying baby doll to Lillian. Wanda leaned down and caressed it. Then she caressed her grown daughter's hair. A cloud eclipsed the moon and the scene was gone.

When the cloud scuttled on and we could see again, Lillian was stepping off our side of the bridge, walking toward us, alone except for the doll cradled in her arms.

We all hugged her and slogged through the mud back toward the store. Thankfully, the flashlights were working again.

Back in the relative safety of the camp store, Bill served us hot chocolate and coffee. "My lights went out for a few moments," he said. "But that worthless radio never warned me at all." He looked at the radio as if it were a new enemy. "Ought to just throw it out," he said. "I thought the wind was going to pick up the whole store and blow me right to Kansas like Dorothy in The Wizard of Oz."

"Do you think it was coincidence that brought us all here tonight, on the very night another storm came and almost washed the bridge away?" I knew what I believed. I just wanted to know what the others thought.

Lillian smiled sadly. "That would be quite a coincidence, wouldn't it? All this happening right after my late father told me the story of my childhood, how he had followed the sound of my tiny one year old voice to the pile of brush beside the creek." She wiped her eyes with the towel Bill had given her. "He said I was calling out for my mama, over and over. Except sometimes, he said it sounded as if I was saying Wanda. As if I were desperately calling her by her true name since she wasn't responding to Mama." She squeezed the old baby doll firmly. Now that Nora was gone, it no longer cried.

"Yep, that is really some coincidence, isn't it?" Mr. Lee said.

"Yeah . . . and if we hadn't stopped by the camp store on our way out, we never would have met." I didn't look at anyone but Jase. He knew what I was getting at. What if we'd been twenty miles down the highway when the storm came? Would Lillian have gone down to the bridge at all?

I liked to think things would have turned out the same. I liked to think that Nora would have found a way to see her, and to save her, even if we hadn't been there. Just like she'd been trying to save her over and over again all these years. Throwing Lillian's old baby doll in the water every time new campers arrived. Waiting to see who would respond. I'll bet some people —the ones who were completely closed off to the spiritual world —never saw or heard a thing.

And then we came along. Right when we were supposed to.

THE TRIP HOME WAS SOLEMN. We left Lillian in the care of Cletus and Bill, and after the cloudburst that had caused the flood, the weather calmed and it was as if it had been just another summer storm. Limbs and branches littered the roadway, and the air was thick with the heavy tang of newly washed pine.

Park trucks were out in force, cutting up the fallen trees and branches and hauling them off the road. In a couple of low spots, water still stood, but it was never so deep that we were afraid to cross. Mr. Lee simply drove slowly through it. We weren't the only family leaving the campground. In fact, it was a mass exodus after the bear and the storm.

I kept waiting for Mr. and Mrs. Lee to start questioning us about Nora and Wanda. But they seemed surprisingly uninterested. Maybe they were in shock. We'd all been there, peering into that driving rain. Is it possible they didn't see the same things we did? I was afraid to ask.

I dozed off and on, my head on Jase's shoulder. Once, I awoke and he was looking at me. I couldn't tell his thoughts, though. The interior of the car was dark and the scant moonlight painted his face with odd gray planes and angles. He didn't look like my Jase at all. He looked like a man, or the man he was becoming.

WHEN WE ARRIVED HOME, the house was dark.

My heart lurched right up into my throat. My fears had come true. Something was wrong. Gramps would've left the lamp on. Even if we had come home a day early, it didn't matter. He would've left the lamp on for me, just in case.

I flew out of the car and up the walk, fumbling for my house key all the way. Finally, I found the string beneath my shirt.

By this time, the Lee family was behind me.

Heart hammering, I flung open the door and the stale air rushed out. I dashed through the rooms turning on lights as I went, calling his name. The living room, bedrooms, even the bathroom, were all empty.

"Here," Jase said. He was standing at the kitchen table, a sheet of notepaper in his hand.

I grabbed it.

"Stevie," the note read. "Your grandpa is in the hospital. He's had a mild heart attack, but he will be okay."

The word okay was underlined in red.

The note continued: "You are welcome to stay with me until he comes home, or you can stay with Ina May Gardner from church—"

"No," Mrs. Lee said, reading over my shoulder. "You will stay with us." She touched my shoulder and all my bones turned to mush.

I sat down heavily. Memories of my grandparents and me at this kitchen table flashed through my mind, unbidden. My worst fears had come home. Worse than the phantoms, worse than the crying doll, worse than Karla, even worse than the bear . . . my Gramps was ill. If I lost him, I would have no one.

Mr. Lee picked up the note from beneath my hand. "Mr. Pearcy wrote this. It says we can call him or go straight to the hospital."

I stood. My legs were shaky, but I started toward the door. "What are we waiting for?"

I made certain the house was locked up, with the lamp left on, and we piled silently into the car for the short ride.

Gramps was in the cardiac intensive care unit. I was the only one allowed to go in. Derol, Pavey's mother, hugged me, hard. She was the nurse on duty. Her white uniform was ghostly in the florescent lighting.

"He's going to be fine," she said. "But it will take some time, and he will have to take it easy." She patted my back. "Don't worry. We're taking good care of him."

Tears sprang to my eyes. "Why didn't someone call me? What if he had—what if he had *died*?" I swiped the tears away angrily. I needed to get myself under control before I went into his room.

Jase appeared beside me with a damp paper towel from the restroom.

I squeezed his hand and dabbed at my face.

"You're not alone," he said, as if he'd read my thoughts. "I'm here. Not going anywhere."

As if to prove his point, he flopped down on the orange Naugahyde sofa in the waiting room. Derol's mom smiled.

"You ready?" she asked.

I looked at Jase sprawled out on the shiny sofa. The lights made his blond hair gleam. He'd gotten very tan while we were at the lake. His parents were talking to a doctor at the nurse's station. All those details meant nothing now. I was just putting off going in.

I drew myself upright and squared my shoulders as if I were gathering up enough courage to go inside the old haunted Taylor mansion again. "Ready," I said.

She took my hand and led me down the hall. Outside a set of wide double doors, we stopped. "He is pale," she said. "And he is hooked up to an intravenous line and heart monitors. Don't worry. He's okay."

I took a deep breath, willing the jittery tears to go away. "Okay." I squeezed her hand and she pushed a large red button on the wall.

The doors swung soundlessly open and we stepped through.

I'd thought we were entering another hall and that there would be rooms on either side, but this was different. We'd stepped into one large open space containing a multitude of beds.

"He's in bed three," Mrs. Pavey said.

The light was dimmer here. Most of the patients were elderly. They appeared to be sleeping; their old mouths open and toothless as chicken beaks. Their snoring was punctuated with the beeps and whooshes of the life-giving machines surrounding them.

I tried to pick my Gramps out of the bed line-up, but they all looked the same.

Panic rose in my chest. "Where is he? I don't see him!"

"Here, right here," Mrs. Pavey said. She led me to the third bed on the left. There was another row of beds on the right.

"Gramps?"

Mrs. Pavey placed my hand on top of his. "He's groggy from

the medications, but he can hear you." She smiled. "I'll be back in a few minutes."

"Stevie-girl," he croaked. He opened his pale blue eyes. *When had they gotten so milky looking?* His bottom teeth were in a glass beside the bed. I'd never seen him without his teeth before. Sometimes he would jokingly poke them out at me, to make me giggle. But he never let anyone see him without them. It made me sad. It scared me worse than all of the wires and tubes put together.

"Gramps." The tears came without warning. I found a straight-backed chair and pulled it over.

He patted my hand. "I'm okay." He started to say more, but I interrupted.

"You should have had someone call me. The ranger could have brought a message—"

He shook his old head slowly. "I knew it was minor," he said. "Didn't want to spoil your first camping trip."

I wiped my face with my crumpled paper towel. It was already dry, scratchy. No way I was going to tell him about the bear. If he realized we were back early, I would have to make something up. I pressed my forehead to the edge of his bed. I was suddenly so tired.

"I've got something for you," he said. "Something I've been saving until you were old enough . . ."

I looked at his face. Even though he was talking, his eyes were closed again. His skin was pasty. The veins in his temples were blue. I rubbed my thumb across his curled fingers. That was about the only place where nothing protruded.

"The cigar box in the top of my closet," he said. "Don't be mad at me for keeping them from you." He opened his eyes and stared directly into mine. "I was only trying to protect you."

"Oh, Gramps." I squeezed his old fingers. "I could never be mad at you."

He squeezed back, weakly. "The box is full of letters from Big Steve." His voice was little more than a whisper.

Mrs. Pavey reappeared. "He needs to rest now, Stevie." She straightened his pillow and checked the flow of medicine dripping from the IV bag on the pole. "You can come back in the morning, first thing." Her tone was bright.

I wondered if that took practice, making yourself sound cheerful all the time, amidst all the sick people. Or maybe it was a skill they taught at nursing school.

I said goodnight to Gramps and kissed him on the forehead, careful not to crimp his IV line when I leaned over the bed. Then I followed Mrs. Pavey obediently.

Jase and his folks stood when we came back through the waiting room doors.

"The doc says it really was a mild one, sort of like a warning," Mr. Lee told me.

I nodded. "I need to go home."

"We can get clean clothes tomorrow," Mrs. Lee said. "I've already called Mr. Pearcy and told him you would be staying at our house."

I looked at the three faces that had become so dear to me over the past week. "Thank you," I said. "I—umm—there's something else I need to get from the house. If you don't mind." I looked to Jase for support. "It won't take but a few minutes."

Jase must've heard the plea in my voice. "I'm sure we can spare a few minutes, can't we, Mom? Dad?" He reached for my hand automatically.

Mr. Lee smiled, resigned. Even though it was almost three o'clock in the morning, he knew when he was out voted. "Sure," he agreed. "Then it's home to bed." He started toward the exit. "What a day this has been."

In the car, I silently went over everything that had happened on this trip: Karla, the bear, the storm, Lillian, and now Gramps.

When I thought of it that way, it made me feel sort of terrified to find out what was written in those letters in Gramps's closet. If it was anything like the rest of this day, it could be wonderful, like helping the ghosts of Wanda and Nora finally locate Lillian, or it could be something positively terrible, like my experiences with Karla and the bear.

r. Lee drove straight back to my house and together we all trooped back up the walk. I was glad I'd left the lamp on. It helped a bit, but not enough. The house still felt empty. It felt so wrong, as if we had all moved on, or as if we hadn't been there at all.

I was glad when everyone came in with me, again. "I'll only be a minute," I said. "Gramps asked me to get something out of his closet."

Mrs. Lee looked a bit concerned, as if she'd heard something in my voice. But she nodded and motioned for the others to sit down and give me my space.

In the bedroom, I went straight to his closet and pulled the string that turned on the bare bulb in the ceiling. The box wasn't hard to spot. Gramps was a real neat freak. A place for everything, and everything in its place, that was his motto.

The cigar box was right there on the top shelf. His old straw hat was upside down on top of it. I stood on my tiptoes, but I couldn't quite reach it. I looked around for something to stand on, but there was nothing. I'd just made up my mind to go to the utility room and fetch the stepstool when I felt someone behind me.

I turned and met Jase's eyes.

"Need some help?" he asked.

I nodded and pointed at the box.

He reached over my head and pulled it down with ease.

The box was a smooth yellow rectangle. The red Roi-Tan cigar label was still visible on the lid. I knew the inside of the box would smell like tobacco. These boxes were the best treasure receptacles in the world. They were sturdy and the lid fit down just perfectly. I kept two in my room. One held hair ribbons and school awards. The other held scraps of paper and trinkets my mom had left behind. Even her old keys were in there.

"What is it?" Jase asked.

"It's a box of letters." I couldn't control the tremor in my words. "From my dad." I sat on the edge of the bed and looked at my best friend. "I'm afraid to read them." Gramps's blue chenille bedspread was pulled up, the pillow tucked neatly inside. I had a moment to wonder where he'd been when the heart attack had struck. The house was as neat as ever. Maybe it had happened at work.

"Want me to do it?" Jase sat on the bed beside me.

I realized my mind had been wandering, probably trying to avoid having to deal with the moment. I tucked the tip of my braid into the corner of my mouth. "I don't know if I even *want* to read them." I held the box tightly. "Maybe it's better not to know. I mean, I've gotten along okay till now . . ." Gramps had said he was keeping the letters secret to protect me. *What did I need protecting from?*

Jase waited patiently. He didn't point out the obvious reason that Gramps was giving them to me now. Instead, he said, "It's been a long day. We could get some sleep and read them tomorrow."

I nodded slowly. We *could* do that. I would probably feel better after some rest, besides, I needed to get to sleep so I could get up and go back to the hospital tomorrow. Plus, I had to think about Mr. Lee. He had driven the whole way home. He hadn't napped in the car the way the rest of us had. *He must be exhausted.*

That thought settled it. "Okay," I said. "Let's take them with us and read them tomorrow." I tucked the box under my arm.

MRS. LEE HAD LEFT the porch light on at their house. There was also a big light on the front of the barn where Buddy lived.

I was yawning the whole way from my house to the Lee's house. But when we turned into their drive, I felt that dread settle in again.

"There's Buddy," Jase said.

The palomino was standing between the house and the barn. His coat looked velvety in the moonlight. He turned his head toward us as we drove up the curved drive. Must've heard our tires on the gravel.

When we climbed out of the car, he trotted toward the fence, whinnying.

"He's been lonesome," Jase said. He went straight to the fence. Buddy was hanging his head over the top rail, waiting for a nose-rub. "Hey, Bud," I heard Jase whisper.

I smiled. How nice it must be to have someone there to greet you. For a fleeting moment, I experienced a deep pang of longing. *Why had we never gotten that dog we'd talked about?* Then directly on the heels of that thought: *Who would be taking care of it now, if we had?*

We unloaded the car and carried the camping equipment

into the garage. "We'll sort it out after we've had some sleep," Mr. Lee said.

We all stumbled into the house, single file. I was still clutching the box of letters. Mr. and Mrs. Lee had looked at the box questioningly when Jase and I returned to the living room back at my house, but they never voiced their concerns. I was amazed at that. If the roles had been reversed, my Gramps would have been on that box like a rooster on a snake.

"It's some letters Gramps was saving for me," I explained. I thought it would be rude not to say something. After all, they had gone out of their way to take me back to get them.

Mrs. Lee nodded politely, but didn't pry. "I hope you don't mind sleeping in Rusty's room." She guided me into the bedroom and turned down the spread as she spoke.

"I don't mind, if you don't," I replied. I hoped she understood what I meant.

Her eyes were very tired when she turned her face toward me. "No," she said. "And I know Rusty wouldn't mind." Her smile was sad.

I didn't even try to resist my nature. I just walked up and gave her a hug. We'd been through so much on this trip, I no longer felt as if she was simply Jase's mom, now I knew her as a real person.

"You are such a dear little thing," she said, patting my back.

I didn't know whether to say thank you or what, so I didn't say anything at all.

"The fresh towels are in the cupboard beneath the sink." She turned to go. "In case you feel like freshening up."

I nodded. Now I could say it. "Thank you. Thanks for everything you and Mr. Lee have done for me."

She just waved her hand at me and paused in the doorway. "You're like one of the family, Stevie." Then she went out the door and I plopped down on the bed, my cigar box still tucked under my arm. My gaze traveled all around the room. I'd glanced inside a few times, as I was going down the hall to the bathroom or what-have-you, but this was the first time I'd ever actually been inside, sitting on the bed.

One wall held football and baseball trophies. Rusty had been a big deal in high school. The sports trophies were on special display shelves. I figured Mr. Lee had built them himself.

"Hey." Jase poked his head in the door. "You doing okay?"

I tried to smile. "Just looking at Rusty's trophies."

"He was such an athlete." Jase let his eyes wander to the trophy wall, too.

I wondered if he realized he'd used the past tense in that sentence. As if his brother was already gone.

"He should have been in college," Jase said. He pushed the blond hair off his forehead. "If he hadn't taken a year off to drive across the country with his buddies, he probably wouldn't have been drafted. College students usually get deferred."

That was new information to me. Hadn't Jase said *he* wanted to drive across the country like Jack Kerouac? Or was it more like his brother, Rusty? "That's tough," I said. "I didn't know that."

Jase shrugged, but I knew it meant something or he wouldn't have mentioned it. "Want to read them now, or tomorrow?" He indicated the box.

I sat it on the bed and debated opening it. "Tomorrow, I think." Then I laughed. "It's already tomorrow, really." As if on cue, I yawned again. "But I'm too tired to think straight right now."

"Okay. Goodnight, then." He walked across the room, tugged my braid, and dropped a quick kiss on the top of my head. Then he disappeared down the hall toward his own room.

I pulled off my shoes and wondered whether I should just sleep in my clothes. The bed looked so fresh and clean, and I felt so dirty from our trip, I hated to mess it up.

"Knock, knock." It was Jase again. "Here's your overnight case in case you wanted anything." He placed it just inside the door and turned away again.

"Thanks," I called softly.

He stopped. "It was a heck of a trip, wasn't it?" His voice was almost as soft as mine.

"I'll never forget it, that's for sure." We looked at each other, a silent something passing between us like a shared thought. I recalled our first real kiss, sitting by the cold campfire, wrapped up in his scratchy blanket. That seemed like a dream to me now. He turned and went on to his room.

I dug out my toothbrush and quickly visited the bathroom. I didn't want to think about stuff too much. Things were going to change now. How much, I just wasn't sure.

AFTER I RETURNED to Rusty's room, I put on my pajamas and crawled between the blessedly cool sheets. Rusty's curtains were blue and maroon plaid. They filtered the moonlight almost completely. I crawled to the end of the narrow bed and pulled the curtains open just enough so the moonlight could slip inside. It lay on the coiled blue rug like a promise. There, I thought. Now I can go to sleep.

But I was wrong. I'd placed the box of letters on the nightstand, and when I reached over to turn off the lamp, my hand brushed the box and before I knew what I was doing, I had the lid up and had spilled the envelopes all over the plaid counterpane.

Dear Stevie, the first one read:

I'm so sorry I'm not there for you. I should never have taken off the way I did. Me and your Mom had a fight. She didn't like me drinking and I thought I should be able to do whatever I wanted.

It's my fault she's gone, Stevie-girl. I take the full blame. If she hadn't been searching for me, she would still be alive.

I laid the letter down. It was written on thin, cheap, paper which was so creased with age it folded itself back into thirds as soon as I released the edges. I took a deep breath and turned the envelope over. The return address had his name, a long number, and the address of a detention center near Amarillo. The postage stamp was pale, but it appeared to have been mailed a few months after my mom's death.

Turning back to the letter, I marveled at the fact that the spiky blue script had actually been written by my father, a man I hadn't seen since I was a little kid. A man who was more of a myth than a memory.

I picked it up and opened the folds again.

I hope you can find it in your heart to forgive me, the letter continued. I've been nothing but selfish my whole life, and look where it's gotten me. I'm in prison, Stevie. I'll be here for a long, long time.

You deserve better.

If I don't hear from you, I'll understand. But I won't give up on you. I hope you don't give up on me, either.

Love,

Big Steve, your dad

I LOOKED AT THE DOOR. Was Jase still awake? What would he think of this letter?

Folding it gently, I slipped the page back into its envelope and put it aside. There were at least twenty letters, maybe even more. He must have written me two or three times a year, every year. For a moment, I did feel a flash of anger that Gramps had kept them from me. Then it was gone. *What good would it have done to know he was in prison?* As soon as that thought crossed my mind, another followed it: *What was he in prison for? Is he still there?*

I picked up the next letter, and then decided I'd better read them in order. When I'd spilled them onto the bed, they'd gotten mixed up. I picked them up, one by one, and began to organize them by the dates they were posted. By the time I was done with that, my eyes were blurry with fatigue. But I couldn't stop.

It took over an hour, but I read every single letter one after the other, devouring them as if they were chocolates in a heart shaped box.

Some I had to read twice.

14

"What did they say?" Jase asked the next day, after his parents were out of earshot.

We were standing at the kitchen sink, washing the breakfast dishes even though it was nearly noon. Mr. and Mrs. Lee said they were going to the garage to straighten out the camping gear. They assured me they would take me back to the hospital as soon as I was ready.

"How'd you know I read them?" I hadn't told him anything.

"How could you not read them?" His voice was incredulous. "No way I could have them right beside me and *not* read them, that's for sure."

I nodded, absent-mindedly squeezing soap bubbles through my palms as I thought about all those letters. "He's in prison," I said. "Near Amarillo. Right where my mom was headed when she collided with that semi."

Jase leaned his side against mine without saying anything. He was warm. It gave me strength somehow.

"He was in jail up there for driving drunk—DWI." I looked through the Lee's kitchen window into the backfield where Buddy grazed solemnly. It was there, two years earlier that the pilot, Roger Gilpin, had tried to land his small plane in a high wind. But I wasn't really seeing the field, or thinking about the phantom pilot. I was seeing my dad behind bars, my mom on a stretcher being loaded into an ambulance on a lonely highway.

I rubbed my wrist across my face, careful not to get soap bubbles in my eyes. "It was his third time for driving drunk. They sent him right to prison. I guess he was on probation or something . . . anyhow, Mom was headed there, but of course she didn't make it."

I leaned my head sideways against Jase's shoulder. "He's still there."

Jase turned and wrapped his arms around me while I whimpered into his shirtfront.

"I have to go see him."

"I'll go with you," Jase said.

I shook my head. "I don't know. I have to think about it." I dried my face on his shirt, but I didn't look up. This was something I needed to say. I wasn't sure I could say it if he was looking at me. "He wasn't hiding from me like I thought. He was writing me every year on my birthday and at Christmas, and sometimes other letters, too. He does love me, he always has. I think he loved Mom, too. Even though they argued." I cleared my throat. I could feel Jase wanting to say something, but I wasn't done. "He said he's sorry for how badly he messed things up, so he just left it up to Gramps whether I ever got those letters. He said he feels like I'm probably better off without him. He also says he'll keep writing me anyway, and that I shouldn't give up on him, no matter what." Finally, I inhaled.

"Wow." Jase's voice was subdued. "When was the last letter written?"

I looked up at him. The bright sunlight streaming through the window seemed suddenly out of place. I felt as if it should be nighttime, or winter. "Two weeks ago." I chewed my bottom lip since I couldn't reach my braid. "I've got to get up to the hospital now." I hugged my best friend quickly. "I feel like I'm in limbo." I looked into his green eyes once more. "And I don't like the feeling."

"Yeah, that's just the way it feels not knowing about Rusty. Limbo."

We bonked foreheads gently, understanding complete.

GRAMPS WAS awake when I went in this time. But he really didn't look that much better, just awake.

"Stevie-girl." He held up the hand that was not attached to the IV pole.

I sat in the same chair as before. I tried not to let my emotions show. Derol's mom wasn't here this time. It was my assumption that she was on the night shift. The other nurse looked at me sternly. She said I was not allowed to upset Gramps.

I didn't know her and she didn't know me. That upset *me* for some reason. I guess I wanted to think that Gramps was in the care of friends, not just in the hospital.

"I'm staying with Jase's family," I said by way of greeting. "How are you feeling?"

He grinned. "Ready to get out of here and go back to work." His hand squeezed mine. I told myself it was stronger than before.

The silence was awkward. I wasn't sure how that could be, I mean, this was my Gramps, after all. Nevertheless, it felt wrong. I fidgeted in my seat.

"You read those letters yet?" His voice was tan, nondescript. It sort of fit this place. It sounded sterile.

I nodded. "Yes sir, I read them all."

"You mad at me?" His grip tightened.

"No. I almost was, but then I realized why you didn't show them to me. I was too young to understand." I squeezed back, very gently, to let him know everything was all right. "I get it now, though."

Gramps closed his eyes and sighed. "Girl, you are something else. I can't believe you're not mad at me. But I'm glad."

The room was still for a while, except for the sounds of the machines. I began to feel comfortable again. No matter what had happened, this was still my Gramps. It would be okay. We could still talk.

"Are you going to write him back?"

I hesitated. "I might go see him," I said. "What do you think about that?"

Gramps opened his eyes and looked at the ceiling. "I thought you might. He has a sister near there. I had Mr. Pearcy call her for me. She will meet you when you decide to go."

I was dumbfounded. "I have an aunt?"

The nurse stuck her head in the door. "Ten minutes are up, folks." Her voice was as stern as the look she'd given me earlier. "Patients need their rest."

Gramps waved his hand at her as if to tell her to lighten up. If he'd said *Pshaw*, I would've giggled. It was one of his favorite words.

The nurse furrowed her brow and glared at him.

"I'd better go." I stood, still holding his hand. "I'll be back tonight when the next visiting hours come." In the cardiac care unit, patients were only allowed visitors for ten minutes in the morning—which I had missed because we'd slept in—then again in the afternoon, and once more in the evening. Last night Mrs. Pavey had made an exception for me since I'd just gotten back.

"Mr. Pearcy has the number if you want to call your aunt," he said.

I placed his hand back onto the bed. "I wonder why she never contacted me." I wanted to ask, but I didn't want to appear to be pushing, so I just said it like that.

"I had Mr. Pearcy ask her that very question."

His blue eyes didn't look quite so milky today. I thought that was a sure sign he was recovering.

"Know what she said?"

I shook my head. My braid flipped from one shoulder to the other.

"Said she was afraid you'd blame her because she's the one who told your mom where to find Big Steve."

My face must have mirrored my confusion.

"She told your mom that your dad was in jail—if not for that, your mom might not have taken off toward Amarillo to see him."

Understanding dawned on me. "So she feels guilty because that's when Mom got killed, huh?"

Gramps nodded. "You can never be certain what a person is thinking unless you ask."

I let that bit of wisdom slide by. Later, I would examine it closer—it sounded kind of profound, like his old saying about being thankful for what you've got, even if it's lukewarm, not hot. Country wisdom, he called it.

"But, will she even want to see me? Or will I just make her feel worse?" Already I was trying to picture her in my head. *Had I ever met her? Did she look like my dad? It had been so long—would I even recognize my dad if I saw him?*

"Gramps?"

The nurse was standing at the door now, holding it open with one hand, making a show of glancing at her watch.

"Stevie?" Gramps always did that to me, just to tease.

I smiled. "Do we have any pictures of my dad? I have a couple of Mom, but none of him." I glanced at the nurse. She was frowning right at me. I started toward her, slowly.

"Look in the frame on the TV. Their wedding picture is in there." He looked at the nurse, too. She glanced away for a second.

"That's my school picture . . ." I could visualize that picture as plain as day. Each year, Gramps took my new picture and changed it out with the one from last year. That 8x10 frame had sat on the TV for as long as I could remember.

"Behind it," Gramps said. "In the same frame. I was going to throw it out—I was so angry with your dad after your mom died —but I couldn't do it. I knew you'd want it, someday."

15

Sitting on a bench in the Greyhound Bus station in Crossroads, I asked Jase what he thought about my bear. "Do you think it was real? Or just part of Wanda's attempt to get us to leave them alone so she could go on searching for baby Lillian?"

Jase took my braid and tucked the end of it in *his* mouth.

We both laughed and I pulled it away.

"I think it was all part of some greater plan," he said. "Just like Karla arriving out of the blue like that—who would've ever thought that would happen?"

"Or that she would have changed so much." I felt myself scowling at the awful memory.

Jase nodded in sympathy. "All the little pieces just fell together, didn't they? Like the hand of Fate, finishing some old cosmic jigsaw puzzle." He grinned and gave my braid one final tug as if to say the matter was closed.

"Do you think my Gramps will be okay?" Now my voice was small. It was the one question I was really afraid to ask.

Jase was quiet. His parents were out in the car, waiting patiently. They said they would come inside in a moment. I think they were just giving us some private time to say goodbye. "I think he will be okay," Jase said at last. "I know he won't be the same as before. He'll need help for awhile at least, but we will all be here for him."

"And he has Mr. Pearcy and the ladies from the church." I looked away. I should be the one taking care of him. It should be me. I should just turn around and go home. Gramps needs me.

The man behind the ticket counter leaned over and spoke into a microphone. "Bus to Amarillo. Bus to Amarillo." He stood, walked around his desk, and came through a door beside the ticket window. "Have your ticket ready if you're going to Amarillo." His voice was singsong. I could tell this was old hat to him. He must've done it a thousand times before.

My knees were shaking. I had decided to go to Amarillo to see my father. The letters said he just wanted to explain everything to me in person.

I picked up my small case. My other suitcase was already on the bus. A few moments earlier, we had watched the driver and another man load the luggage into the big compartment underneath the middle of the huge bus. The chilly morning air had made their breath puff out in front of their mouths like little dialogue bubbles in a comic strip. I wanted nothing more than to go back in time to our cheerful kitchen, make myself a glass of chocolate milk, and think of things to write in those little bubbles. I would put Janis Joplin on the stereo and then I would take a pad of sketch paper and a charcoal pencil just like the ones we'd had in Art class at Crossroad's Junior High. I would sketch that bus and those men. That's how I would pass the few minutes while I waited for Gramps to come through the door after work. That's how I would be sitting when Jase knocked once, and then came on in. That's how I would always be, in my memories.

Mr. and Mrs. Lee materialized by my side as if by magic.

They hugged me tightly, one after the other. "Be safe," Mrs. Lee said.

I won't cry. I won't!

Mr. Lee pressed a twenty-dollar bill and a roll of quarters into my hand. "You call us when you get there, young lady. There'll be a payphone in the station." His voice was rough. "Let us know everything's all right."

I nodded. "Thank you. I will." Tears were really threatening now, so I turned away.

"I wish you'd just let us drive you," Jase said for the umpteenth time. 'I'd feel better if you weren't going alone."

I shook my head. "Sometimes it's better to face things by yourself. Besides, my Dad's sister is going to meet me at the station." I gave the clerk my ticket.

Jase stepped through the outside door with me. The bus was idling at the curb. People were climbing on, silently, their bare hands grasping the silver handrails on either side of the door as they pulled themselves up the three steep steps. Most of my fellow travelers were older than me. I began to scout their faces, picking out the ones I wouldn't mind sitting by, in case the bus was full.

Suddenly, I was certain this was a mistake. Who cares if my father wants to see me? I've wanted to see him for years.

I was on the verge of backing out.

We were so close to boarding, I could see that the steps were coated with a black rubber mat containing dozens of tiny grooves. In the sunlight, those grooves sparkled with years of accumulated bits of crushed hard candies and other debris. A cellophane wrapper from a pack of cigarettes glittered under the driver's seat.

It was almost my turn.

Jase grabbed my hand and stopped me.

I wanted to protest. My courage was almost gone.

Then he did something unexpected. He opened my hand, planted a slip of paper directly into the palm, and then folded my fingers down over it. With a quick jerk of his head, he flopped the thick hank of hair out of his eyes. I knew I would replay that gesture in my mind more than once in the coming days.

His voice held a note of urgency. "That's for when you get scared or lonely," he whispered. "You can read it later."

Tears blurred my vision.

Darn him!

He took my face in his hands, made me look up at him, and then he said, "And this is for when you need to know you are loved." He kissed me quickly, right on the lips, right there in front of God and everybody.

I kept my eyes closed and let the tears flow.

"And, Stevie-girl—"

I looked at him.

"—don't get up there to Amarillo and forget to come back home."

I must have looked confused.

"He may be your father, but we're your family."

I hugged him tightly and stumbled up the three steps, tears blurring my vision completely.

The bus was a hundred miles down the road before I was finally able to release my grip on the crumpled slip of paper long enough to read it.

I recognized Jase's handwriting immediately.

"You and me," it said simply. "Don't forget."

As if I ever could.

ABOUT THE AUTHOR

Ann Swann is the author of *Stevie-girl and the Phantom Pilot*, and *Stevie-girl and the Phantom Student*, books one and two of The Phantom Series, which was originally published by Cool Well Press. She has also written numerous award winning short stories and novels for adults. She lives in West Texas with her husband and their rescue pets. She loves libraries and book stores and owns two different e-readers just for fun.

How to Contact Ann Swann:
Amazon Central: http://tinyurl.com/6wl3oe2
Blog: www.annswann.blogspot.com
Email: swannann76@yahoo.com
Goodreads: http://tinyurl.com/6vuw7vl

OTHER TITLES FROM 5 PRINCE PUBLISHING

www.5princebooks.com

Never Saw It Coming *Bernadette Marie*
Blissful Disaster *Amy L. Gale*
Victory *Bernadette Marie*
Chasing Her Heart *J. L. Petersen*
Alone *M.J. Kane*
Hope in the Rain *Sandy Sinnett*
The Deja Vu House *Doug Simpson*
We Are From Atlantis *Doug Simpson*
Prez *Lissa Jay*
The Train Robbers *James P Hanley*
Walker Revenge *Bernadette Marie*
Lest We Aren't Forgiven *Railyn Stone*
Broken Hearts *M.O. Kenyan*
Goodnight Kisses *Wilhelmina Stolen*
The Three Stones of Bethany *April Marcom*
Wanderlust *Bernadette Marie*
Holiday Past *Jessica Dall*
Christmas Blitz *Amy Gale*